COPYRIGHT PAGE

Copyright © 2020 by Vella Day
www.velladay.com
velladayauthor@gmail.com
Edited by Rebecca Cartee and Carol Adcock-Bezzo

Published in the United States of America

E-book ISBN: 978-1-951430-04-7
Print book ISBN: 978-1-951430-05-4

ALL RIGHTS RESERVED. No part of this book may be used or reproduced in any manner whatsoever without written permission of the author except in the case of brief questions embodied in critical articles or reviews.

This is a work of fiction. Names, characters, places, and incidents either are the product of the author's imagination or are used fictitiously, and any resemblance to actual persons living or dead, business establishments, events or locales, is entirely coincidental.

PINK IS THE NEW BLACK

A PARANORMAL COZY MYSTERY

A WITCHS COVE MYSTERY
BOOK ONE

VELLA DAY

EROTIC READS PUBLSIHING

ABOUT THE BOOK

An inept witch. A talking pink iguana. A town trying to solve a lawman's murder.

Hi, I'm Glinda Goodall—the Good Witch of the South—and I want to welcome you to Witch's Cove, Florida, a delightful beach town where witches and humans reside in peace and harmony. Sounds perfect, right? Yeah, that's what it says on the billboard, but here's the real scoop.

My aunt, who runs the Tiki Hut Grill where I work, sees ghosts—or rather sees one of them—namely her dead husband. My mom, a funeral director, is addicted to all things that have to do with The Wizard of Oz. She even has a terrier named Toto. And then there's my familiar, Iggy, who is a very disgruntled pink iguana who fancies himself a detective.

As for me, I'm a problem solver. My flaws are that I'm way too nosy for my own good, and I rarely say the right thing at the right time.

This week's exciting news? Our not-so-beloved law

enforcement officer was murdered, and my best friend's brother was accused of the crime. I have to help find the real killer, right? How could I not?

Stop in to Witch's Cove and grab a meal at the Tiki Hut Grill. You just might see me and my familiar in action.

CHAPTER 1

"Glinda, can you take table eight? Penny has an emergency phone call," Aunt Fern called from behind the restaurant's cashier's counter.

When I looked over and saw that Sheriff Duncan and his creepy son, Cliff, were sitting there, I held in a groan but painted on a smile. "Sure thing!"

It wasn't as if I could say no. After all, my Aunt Fern owned the Tiki Hut Grill. I had no real beef with Duncan Donut, I mean Sheriff Duncan, but I did with his son, Cliff, his deputy. The guy was always trying to grab a feel or making some snide comment about my outfit. It was none of his business if I liked to wear pink and only pink. It also was none of his business if I had gained weight or not.

With my pad in hand, along with my pink pencil, I weaved my way around a few tables toward the sheriff and his son. Before I could get there though, an arm reached out and stopped me. "Honey, can you refill my coffee?"

I faced him and smiled. When I began waitressing at the Tiki Hut Grill close to three years ago, I was a bit offended by the endearing—or not so endearing—term of Honey, but after a while I got over it. "Sure. Let me get you some."

I'd never seen this man before, but I was happy for the delay. Considering I knew a lot of the residents in Witch's Cove, he had to be a tourist—a tourist we were happy to have.

At the coffee station situated against the south wall of the restaurant, I grabbed a half-full hot pot and rushed back to him. He wasn't sitting at one of my assigned tables, but I served him anyway. Penny, my best girlfriend, was still by the kitchen on the phone. It was her table, but from her serious expression, she might be a while.

Once I poured the man his drink, I hustled over to the sheriff's table. Trying to act professional and not give Cliff any excuse to make a snarky comment, I set the coffee on the empty table next to them and lifted my pad, ready to take their order. Since either the sheriff or Cliff came in here nearly every day, I could guess what each might order. "Hi, Sheriff. The fried cod and French fries with extra gravy?" I asked.

"Sounds perfect. Your Aunt Fern sure has trained you well."

"Thank you." I scribbled down his order. "To drink?"

"It's a bit hot today, so how about some cold lemonade?"

"You got it." Now for creepy Cliff. "For you?"

"You sure are a sight for sore eyes, Glinda. How about a smile for me, darlin'?"

Gag me now. So help me, if he reached out and grabbed me around the hips one more time, I would stab him in the eye with my pencil.

When he lifted his arm, I jumped backward.

"What's gotten into you? Your outfit too tight or something?" He laughed at his own joke.

I eyed the hot pot of coffee a few feet away and was really

tempted to grab it and accidentally on purpose spill it on him. "Everything is peachy, Cliff. A hamburger, medium rare, with all the trimmings?" I asked, wanting to get away from him as quickly as possible.

"You bet." Cliff instantly switched back to his good old boy mode, probably hoping to soften me up. Fat chance of that.

"Do you want a root beer with that meal?"

"You know me so well."

Sadly, too well. Everyone in town was convinced the only reason he had been given the position of deputy was because his father, the sheriff, had appointed him.

His dad leaned back in his seat and nodded toward Aunt Fern. "How's your aunt doing?"

Aunt Fern had lost her husband two years ago and was still grieving. She'd been married to Harold for thirty-years and swore on her pearl necklace that he was still here—as in his ghost visited her every day to chat. I looked over at Aunt Fern, and there she was, bless her heart, talking to the air—I mean to the ghost of Uncle Harold. My mother could communicate with the dead, but she never claimed she could see the person.

"The same. She misses her husband."

"She dating anyone?" the sheriff asked, his eyebrows wiggling in interest.

Really? "I don't know. Why don't you ask her?" I refused to get in the middle of that! Wanting to leave before he asked me to speak to my aunt on his behalf, I spun around, picked up the pot of coffee from the next table, and rushed over to the kitchen to place the order.

As I passed the cashier's counter, Aunt Fern stopped her ghostly chat and turned to me. "Everything okay, Glinda? You look a little peaked."

"Never better." I glanced back over my shoulder, pleased

to see the sheriff and Cliff were in deep conversation. "Heads up. Duncan Donut over there is on the dating warpath again."

Her aunt waved a dismissive hand. "Don't worry about me. I can handle him."

And I bet she could too. Many considered Aunt Fern a bit batty, but I knew better. She was one smart lady.

I placed the lunch order for the sheriff and his son before checking on my other four tables. Penny rushed over and stuffed her phone in her pocket. "Thanks for covering for me. Did Duncan Donut order yet?"

That made me laugh that she'd adopted my nickname for the overly large sheriff. "Yes. Order is in. Everything okay?"

Penny was a single mom with a seven-year old son. "Tommy wasn't feeling well at school, so I had to ask, or rather beg my loser ex-husband to pick up *our* son from school and watch him. He has the day off, so he shouldn't have complained so much."

Sam was a rather unreliable ex-husband who had difficulty when it came to paying child support on time. I rubbed her arm. "I can cover if you want to be with Tommy."

Penny tossed me a weak smile. "I appreciate that, but you've covered enough for me." Her gaze shot to the back entrance that led to the porch. She sucked in a breath and then smiled. "Well lookie who's here."

Being eternally curious, I turned around. "It's Drake!"

I didn't expect to see him this early in the day. Being the proprietor of the Howl at the Moon Cheese and Wine Emporium and its only full-time worker, he never stopped in for lunch unless his assistant, Trace, was working, or if it was Sunday, which was Drake's day off.

Penny touched my arm. "Go chat with him. I'll check on your tables. He looks like the weight of the world is on his shoulders."

"Thanks. I won't be long." Penny knew which tables were mine, since together we had the whole room.

I rushed over to Drake. "Hey, fancy meeting you here, stranger."

"Can we talk?" he asked.

Ooh, that sounded serious. "Sure. Table one is free."

We sat down. Drake and I were both twenty-six and had gone through grade school and most of high school together. No surprise, we became best friends. "What's up?"

"Jaxson's back."

I didn't see that coming. I needed a moment to decide if that was a good thing or a bad thing. Drake's older brother, Jaxson, had been caught robbing the Liquor Mart in town eleven years ago. Once he was convicted, the entire Harrison family moved to Orlando. Then three years ago, Drake returned to Witch's Cove *sans* family. "You don't seem happy about that."

That was slick of me to avoid responding to Jaxson's reappearance. About all I knew for sure was that he'd served his time and then stayed away from Witch's Cove for obvious reasons.

"No, no. I'm happy. Despite what the town thinks, Jaxson is a good guy."

Having wanted to support Drake and his family, I'd gone to the trial. Jaxson claimed he was innocent, and that because he'd caught Sheriff Duncan exiting the back staircase on the outside of the Liquor Mart the night of the robbery, the sheriff painted Jaxson as the bad guy. Drake's brother told the court the sheriff framed him for the robbery. Naturally, the sheriff denied the allegation, saying Jaxson was looking for someone to blame for the theft. I honestly couldn't say who was telling the truth, but the jury agreed with the sheriff.

I inhaled. "Now, what?"

"I'm trying to convince him to stay." Drake looked up and smiled. "Oh, good. Here he is now."

I debated if I should stand and hug Jaxson or remain seated. Because he was six years older than us, I hadn't known him all that well, so I didn't move. Or else I didn't move because I was stunned by the man's transformation. The bonus to his three-year stint in prison was that he was quite buff. The con—no pun intended—was that his eyes looked a bit cold. It was clear that Jaxson Harrison excelled at pulling off the bad boy look.

"Jaxson," I said putting as much cheer in my voice as possible.

His eyes widened slightly as he pulled out a chair and sat down. "My, my if it isn't Glinda the Good Witch. Or are my eyes deceiving me?"

I genuinely smiled. Okay, I hadn't expected such a positive reaction. "It's me! In the flesh." The nickname came about because I am a witch who lives in a beach town on the west coast of Florida. Hence, Glinda the Good Witch of the South.

"You've grown up," he said.

"Well, it's been eleven years."

"So it has. Nice outfit, by the way." Jaxson said and then looked around. "Everyone is in costume, and Halloween isn't for several months. What gives?"

"The costumes were Aunt Fern's idea, and I have to say it's been a boon to business."

He nodded. "The town does seem to be doing well. When I drove in, I didn't see any store closings. That's a far cry from when I was here last."

"Because times were tough back then, the city council decided to make Witch's Cove a tourist destination."

Jaxson laughed. "Other than the sunshine, warm ocean waters, and miles of white sandy beaches, what is the draw?"

I was almost insulted. "Ah, can we say us witches? I mean who wouldn't want to have their fortune told or be able to communicate with a dead relative?"

His eyes sparkled. "I see. I hope it works out."

Penny rushed over, her eyes wide and her face flushed as she drank in Jaxson. "Can I get you guys something to eat or drink?"

The Harrison brothers ordered lunch, while I only wanted a sweet tea.

As we waited for the drinks to arrive, I wanted to address the elephant in the room. "How was prison?" It didn't really matter to me if Jaxson had been released eight years ago.

Drake cleared his throat as Jaxson's eyes narrowed slightly. Whoops. Not the best starter topic, now was it?

"Good. Lots of parties, you know."

I had to laugh. "Sorry. Let me try again. Are you passing through town or are you staying?"

Jaxson looked over at Drake. "I guess that depends on my brother as well as on a few other things."

I wasn't about to ask what that meant exactly, so I looked at Drake for a clue.

"I hope he stays. I told him I could use the help at the store."

"You were serious?" his brother asked.

"Of course, I was. I offered you the job."

"Then I'll certainly consider it." Jaxson faced her.

"I, for one, would love it," I said. "Your brother works really long hours. I almost have to make an appointment just to talk to him."

"I see," Jaxson said rather cryptically.

Just as I was about to ask him another question, Aunt Fern growled, if that was the right word. I looked in her direction only to find Duncan Donut leaning over the cashier's counter, grinning up at my aunt. Oh, boy.

"My Harold would not approve if I went out with anyone," Aunt Fern said in a loud voice.

I couldn't hear the sheriff's response, but he quickly straightened, tossed some cash on the counter, and stalked off. Aunt Fern must have set him straight about her no dating policy. I kind of felt sorry for the sheriff. He seemed lonely too.

When I returned my attention to the lunch guests, Jaxson was glaring at the sheriff. The old saying: *if looks could kill, he'd be dead* would certainly have applied here.

Drake reached across the table and clasped his brother's wrist. "Let it go, Jax. It's in the past."

His brother swung back to face Drake. "Easy for you to say. You didn't have to be cooped up with violent men for three years, all the while knowing the good sheriff had something to do with the robbery that I did time for."

"You have no proof that he was involved in any way," Drake said.

"Doesn't mean he wasn't."

As if some tension-cutting spirits were looking down on us, Penny pranced over with their drinks and grinned. "Here you go. Your food will be right up!"

Oh, my. My best friend had combed her hair and applied fresh makeup. She even seemed to have fixed some of the loose pennies that she'd sewn on her skirt. Someone seemed to be interested in the newcomer.

"Thanks," Jaxson said.

Wanting to help Penny out, I introduced them, and Jaxson was kind enough to look up and smile. "I hope I'll see more of you," he said.

Penny all but burst. "I'd like that."

I was drinking in this blossoming relationship when creepy Cliff stepped over to our table. "What are you doing back in town, Harrison?" His tone was anything but friendly.

Drake must have kicked his brother under the table because my sweet tea shook. "There's no law against visiting my brother, now is there, Cliff?" Jaxson's lip curled.

"No. Just stay out of trouble, you hear?"

Thankfully, Jaxson merely glared at the deputy as Cliff joined his father outside. As soon as he left though, Drake's brother grunted and shoved back his chair so hard it toppled over.

"Whoa. Don't let what he said get to you," Drake said.

"Seriously?" Jaxson shook his head. "I knew it wasn't a good idea to come back here. I should have gone with my gut and never returned."

"What are you going to do now?" Drake asked.

"Get outta of this town. For good."

Drake stood. "Stay a few days at least."

Oh, boy. I'd bet my pink Converse sneakers this wasn't the homecoming either of the Harrison boys anticipated or wanted. Not one to get in the middle of a dispute, I slid back my chair and grabbed my drink.

"I, uh, have to get back to work," I said, happy to have an excuse to leave this stressful situation. If Jaxson left town, it would devastate Drake. "Don't worry about the Duncan men, Jaxson. They're all talk." I tried to sound encouraging, but I think I failed.

Jaxson glared at me and then picked up his chair. "They were doing a lot more than talking the last time I was here. They were framing me!" His voice had escalated enough for the seven occupied tables to quiet.

Okay, that was the signal for me to leave. I tossed Drake a sympathetic look and rushed off to talk to Penny.

CHAPTER 2

Penny was by the coffee station, and as soon as I reached her, she grabbed my arm. "What happened?" she whispered. "Why is Jaxson leaving? He hasn't even eaten yet."

"Cliff was not exactly welcoming." I gave her the low down on what the deputy had said. "I feel sorry for Drake. Unless he goes to visit his brother, they may never see each other again."

She sighed. "That is so sad. Did you know I knew Jaxson in school?"

I did some math in my head. "Well, I'll be. You are both thirty-two, but I'm surprised he didn't recognize you."

Penny's face turned bright red. "I was super skinny in school. And prettier."

I didn't want to hear that nonsense. "You're gorgeous now."

My best girlfriend swept a hand down her penny-covered skirt. "I look ridiculous in this costume."

The last thing I needed was a pity party. "No, you don't. You're Penny Carsted. It's cute that your outfit is covered in pennies. Besides, I bet Jaxson did remember you but thought you didn't know him, which was why he went along with the introduction."

Penny shot a quick glance upward. "Maybe, but he had to know I'd recognize him even if it has been a long time. Who wouldn't remember the hottest guy in school? And those emerald green eyes are to die for." She actually swooned.

"Did you go out with him?"

"Me? No. I'd met Sam a month before that." She chuckled. "I can still remember how jealous he was of Jaxson."

"Jealousy never ends well."

"Tell me about it," she said.

I'd have to remember to ask her about that situation later.

"Oh, Penny?" my aunt called out in a voice loud enough for everyone in the restaurant to hear.

"Hey, I need to go. Don't want to upset your aunt."

"We need to find time to chat," I said.

"Totally."

As soon as Penny took off, I checked on my tables. My shift was from six-thirty in the morning until three in the afternoon, and it was close to two now. When three o'clock finally rolled around, I was very happy to get off my feet. Thankfully, I didn't have far to go to reach home since I lived above the restaurant. The inside stairwell, situated on the far side of the kitchen restaurant, led to two apartments. One was mine, and the other belonged to Aunt Fern. It worked out well, especially since she loved my familiar, Iggy, who I swear liked her better than me. I think that was what prompted her to install two cat doors—one in my front door and one in hers—so Iggy could come and go. She said it was wrong for Iggy to stay cooped up all day.

But actions had consequences. With the new escape route in place, he'd sneak downstairs and talk to Aunt Fern. And yes, I could tell when she was talking to my familiar and when she was *talking* to the ghost of her dead husband.

Why she never decided to have a familiar of her own I don't know. It might be a bit odd for a sixty-three-year old woman to have a familiar this late in life, but I know it would give her comfort.

After I settled up my receipts and refilled all of the condiments for my section, I clocked out. I headed down the back hall and past the kitchen to the flight of stairs that led to my place. If I'd continued past the stairs, I would have ended up in the Tiki Hut clothing and gift shop.

Now that was an interesting place. It had everything from the usual bathing suits and beach paraphernalia to Tiki Hut T-shirts and Tiki Hut tank tops for both men and women. What I didn't care for was the rather tacky, plastic, pink iguanas with our logo on the side. What was even worse was that Aunt Fern had T-shirts made with Iggy's image on it. Why pink? Let me introduce you to my iguana first, and then it will become apparent as to the choice of color.

I climbed the steps to my apartment and let myself in.

Scraping sounds scurried toward me. "About time you got home," Iggy said, lifting his chest high with indignation coloring his tone.

"I'm on the clock with you too?"

Even if I'd come home early, Iggy would complain. To be honest, he had a legitimate beef with me regarding his unorthodox appearance, but after fourteen years, his refrain was getting rather tiresome.

He shot to the sofa, crawled up the side using his sharp nails, and plopped down on the cushion. There wasn't anywhere Iggy couldn't reach. "I heard shouting. What was that about?"

I spun around and faced him. "Were you downstairs?"

If iguanas could shrug, that was what he'd be doing. "Maybe. Okay, yes. I was bored. I wanted to know what was going on."

"Jaxson Harrison returned home for the first time in eleven years. When Cliff was ugly to him, Jaxson decided it would be in his best interest to leave town."

Iggy bobbed his head. "I don't like Cliff."

"That makes two of us."

Iggy jumped down from the sofa, raced over to the window, and hopped up on the stool I'd put there so he could enjoy the water view. Iggy usually only went there when he wanted to contemplate life. When he remained silent, I started to worry.

"What are you thinking?" I asked.

"Are you going to stop Jaxson from leaving?" Iggy finally asked.

"Why do you care?"

He faced me. "I went to the trial too, remember?"

"I do." I'd hidden him in my purse.

"I could tell Duncan Donut was lying on the stand," he said.

"Why didn't you say anything before now?" It was probably because he didn't have any proof, but I wanted to give Iggy the benefit of the doubt. "What was he lying about?"

"He was lying about why he was at the Liquor Mart that night. And I mean the real reason he was there."

Iggy tended to be dramatic. "Okay, Detective Iggy, why was the sheriff there on the night of the robbery?"

"You're too young to have been affected by something so vile, but some men are not faithful."

I did understand that concept, but there was no need to tell him that. Iggy would want to grill me, and that was the last thing I needed today. "And you know this how?"

"Underneath this ugly exterior, I'm all male, and a virile one at that. I know things."

Eww. I so didn't want to go there. "You are not ugly. You're beautiful to me." If not strangely unique. "I have tried many times to reverse the spell that turned you pink, but nothing has worked—obviously. You should be thankful that first spell gave you the ability to talk." It always haunted me that I didn't try hard enough.

All young witches who desired a familiar went into the Hendrian forest, located about five miles outside of town, to summon one. I probably wasn't concentrating hard enough when I imagined a small kitten, because instead of some cute black cat, out pranced an iguana—and a pink one at that. Had I not had my obsession with wearing pink all day every day, Iggy might not have turned that color.

"You're right. I should put what happened in the past— but I can't, or rather I won't." He swooshed his long, striped tail back and forth. "Back to Jaxson's situation. All I'm saying is look into where the sheriff really was the night of the robbery."

"Hello! That was eleven years ago. The trail will be cold." I went into the kitchen to fix myself something to drink, thinking that would end our discussion. Iggy didn't go off the deep end too often, but when he did, it could be a long night.

"Doesn't mean you should ignore the facts," he said, prancing in after me.

I was afraid to ask, but my curious mind made me. "Why do you suspect him again?"

"Let's just say I hear things."

Iggy did have a way of wandering around the restaurant, picking up on the juiciest of gossip. Aunt Fern said when Iggy started to mingle with the clientele many years ago, some customers thought he was dangerous. To prevent anyone from totally freaking out when they spotted my pink lizard, I put a pink rhinestone collar on him. And yes, he hated it, but as I said, I only do pink. Since then, tourists have actually come just to see him. I swear his ego has grown bigger with each passing day.

That might be why I really wasn't in the mood for him tonight. I was still worried about Drake. "How about some TV? That might get your mind off of things," I said.

"Better yet, why don't you talk to Drake? I bet he looked into the sheriff's alibi back then."

"He would have told me. We are besties, don't forget, but Drake was only fifteen at the time. Neither of us really comprehended much back then."

"Then talk to his parents."

"His parents live in Orlando." Okay, something was going on with him. "Why are you so interested in this?"

"I like Drake and want you to be happy. You'd make a cute couple."

So that was what this was all about. I didn't have the heart to tell Iggy that Drake never was nor ever would be interested in me. He'd set his sights on a different lifestyle.

"Fine. I'll camp out at Drake's for a bit and see if we can figure out about how to convince Jaxson to stay."

"Good. I'll do a little investigating myself. I want to know the real truth about Duncan Donut."

I knew that tone. "You will not leave this building," I said in my sternest tone.

Iggy's mouth opened. "Fine."

Not that I trusted him to do as I asked, but I did want to talk to Drake. He had to be hurting with his brother's visit being cut short. If my friend hurt, then so did I.

After I changed out of my uniform, I exited the building through the clothing and gift shop. Between the businesses and the water's edge ran a ten-foot wide pedestrian walkway.

While I have never measured it, it had to be a good half-mile to a mile long. Once outside, I turned right and walked past my parent's funeral home, which sat next to Drake's Wine and Cheese shop. The ocean waves weren't in the best of moods this afternoon. They crashed against the shore, acting as if a storm was coming, and we certainly didn't want any of those. That would be really bad for business. Besides, hurricane season wasn't for another month, and the weather should respect the calendar.

Drake's two-story store had two entrances. The half that faced Coven's Pathway was the main entrance. It was where one could pick from a vast array of cheeses from the cooler and then select the type of crackers to go with it. He also had a host of baskets on display that he would fill with the customer's selection. Drake was a design genius when it came to picking the right combination of cheeses and wine to go in the perfect basket.

In the back was the wine section. That was where I found Drake. "Hi," I said.

He looked up from one of his famous creations. "Hey. Did your aunt send you over for some wine?" He sounded so despondent, I wanted to hug him, but I thought it best not to.

There were two bars at the Tiki Hut grill—the official Tiki Hut that sat on the sand, and the one inside where the clientele could face the ocean from the comfort of an air-conditioned space. When we only needed a few bottles, my aunt bought them from Drake. "No. I came to talk about Jaxson."

"What about me?" his brother said as he exited the side door that led to a storage room.

I was excited to see he hadn't left yet, but from his dour expression, he probably wasn't going to stay long. "This might sound crazy, but Iggy has a theory."

Jaxson's chuckle held little joy. "What does the little bugger have to say?"

Iggy wasn't merely a little bugger. He was my familiar. "For starters, he believes you didn't rob the liquor store."

Jaxson put down the bottle of wine he'd been carrying. "Smart little Iggy. Go on."

"He believes—and I'm interpreting here—the reason the sheriff was at the Liquor Mart the night of the robbery was because he was meeting a woman for illicit purposes." I'd had to draw a few conclusions from Iggy's comments.

Drake's face scrunched up. "A woman would sleep with the sheriff?"

"Be nice." Since only those with magic could hear Iggy, I appreciated that Drake and Jaxson didn't make fun of me because I could.

I looked over at Jaxson. "Why do you think Duncan Donut was there so late at night?"

"I don't know, but I swear the sheriff knew who really robbed the store and was protecting him. I could see it in his eyes."

That was an interesting take, one that hadn't been brought up at trial. Considering Jaxson was in the process of crossing the street when he spotted the sheriff, I doubt he could even see his eyes. "Do you have any idea who robbed the liquor store?" I asked.

"No, but the only one who comes to mind is Cliff."

I chuckled. "Really?" Prison had made Jaxson a bitter and desperate man.

"Cliff is arrogant enough to think he could get away with it," Jaxson said.

"Okay, you have a point, but he is sworn to uphold the law, not break it."

"You're naïve, Glinda, if you believe Cliff would care about that," Jaxson said.

He was just bitter—or at least I hoped what he claimed wasn't true. "Do you really think the sheriff would cover for Cliff if he had been the thief? Duncan Donut is rather straight-laced."

"Parents always—or almost always—do or say what they need to in order to protect their kids. Where do you think the saying, blood is thicker than water, comes from? We know he likes Cliff. Why else would he appoint his son as his deputy? Everyone knows Cliff is a hot head with few analytical skills to solve a crime."

"True." It was concepts like these that made me happy to be a waitress and not a sleuth. I ran my hand down the neck of the bottle that was on the counter. "You said you saw the sheriff at nine p.m., yet Rich Paloma, the Liquor Mart owner, said he was robbed at nine twenty." I had no idea why the details of the crime were burned into my brain.

"Exactly, which means it couldn't have been me. Sure, I went into the Liquor Mart after I spotted the sheriff, but that was to buy some beer. I went straight home after that, only I had no witness to corroborate my story."

"I remember that." Too bad Witch's Cove never wanted security cameras on the streets or Jaxson might not have been accused in the first place. While the interior of the Liquor Mart had cameras, Rich had forgotten to turn them on. I thought that was a bit fishy. "The sheriff claimed you were casing the joint while you were buying beer and then robbed it shortly thereafter."

"All a lie. Rich said the thief wore a mask. The case was rigged. The only evidence was his word against mine."

"Why do you think Duncan Donut targeted you?" I asked.

"I'm sure Drake filled you in on my escapades over the years. I got into a few scrapes every now and again. Not only that, Cliff and I didn't see eye to eye."

"Don't forget," Drake said, "you repeatedly trounced him in wrestling. His dad's pride was continuously wounded."

Jaxson stood up taller. "I won because I was the better wrestler."

"Cliff might not see it that way," Drake said.

Jaxson huffed. "Listen. I'm beat. I'm going back to your place and crash. I plan to head out in the morning."

Darn it. She'd caused more strife. "Jaxson, don't leave on my account. I was only trying to help."

He ran a hand down my arm. "I know, but this town will always see me as an ex-con. They have no interest in learning the truth about the robbery." He turned back to Drake. "I'm sorry."

As soon as Jaxson left, I wanted to apologize to Drake, but what could I say? I shouldn't have brought up his robbery charges, but I couldn't help it. I leaned against the counter where Drake had been putting the finishing touches on the basket. "He may change his mind and stay." That was weak.

"Doubtful. For the most part, this town is incredibly accepting of everyone but my brother. Heck, they welcome witches and people who see ghosts. But ex-cons? Apparently, not."

"It's just Cliff who dislikes your brother. And maybe the sheriff too." Though I had no idea how many others thought the same way.

"I don't trust Cliff. If my brother stays, who knows whether the sheriff or his son would try to frame Jaxson for something else?"

I let out a long sigh. "I get it, and I don't blame Jaxson for wanting to leave. I know you're bummed about it too."

"I am."

"Whether Jaxson robbed the store or not, he's done his time," I said, upset a few of the town's people weren't open-minded. "He deserves a fresh start."

"You're preaching to the choir, my little pink friend."

"Why do you think the sheriff was behind the Liquor Mart that night?"

"You aren't going to let this go, are you?"

I didn't know why Drake asked. He knew the answer. "No."

Drake pushed the basket he was working on aside and leaned his elbows on the counter. "Don't you remember he said he was doing rounds?"

Which was a plausible considering it was his job to patrol the area. Iggy's comment about infidelity came back to me. "Have you met Rich Paloma's wife? Or rather his ex-wife?" They used to live above the Liquor Mart.

"I might have seen her around town every once in a while, but she's never shopped here. Why?"

"Maybe the sheriff and she were, you know…"

Drake groaned. "I suppose anything is possible. Duncan was an eligible bachelor, but Mrs. Paloma was not a single woman at the time."

I cringed to think about the sheriff and her together. "In the eleven years since the conviction, I was hoping Jaxson might have remembered seeing something, something he didn't remember during the trial."

"He has his theories, but he never could substantiate anything," Drake said.

"Then he should stay here and help investigate."

Drake laughed. "And what? Be thrown in jail again for asking too many questions?"

"Fine. Then maybe it's time I run into the former Mrs. Paloma and ask her what happened that night."

"Glinda, no."

Drake always was the overly protective type. "Hilary Paloma is not dangerous."

He held up a hand. "Let's suppose she and the good sheriff

were *friendly* back then. Why would she say anything now? I know it's only rumors, but I've heard Rich Paloma is not the nicest guy. Even after this long, he might take it out on her if he found out. Not only that, but Hilary has a new husband now."

"Darn. You might be right. So, what do we do?"

"I'm sure you'll figure something out."

CHAPTER 3

That night, after I was certain Aunt Fern had enough time to settle in, I knocked on her door. "It's me."

She opened up a minute later. Her hair was in those pink, spongy hair rollers, and she was wearing a purple flannel robe with orange fluffy slippers. "Glinda, this is a nice surprise. Come in."

"Am I interrupting anything?"

"No, no. Of course not. I was just complaining to Harold about our sheriff."

I tried not to react. "Complaining about what?"

"Sheriff Duncan keeps asking me out, and I can't seem to get through to him that I have no interest in dating."

"I'm sure Uncle Harold would understand if you wanted to go out again." Not really, but I wanted to be supportive of my aunt finding happiness.

"That may be, but not with the likes of Duncan Donut. The man is unethical, and I've heard he was involved with a married woman a while back."

Whoa. That was the second time today someone had accused him of that. I wondered why this was the first I'd heard of it. I didn't think I lived under a rock. "Have you been talking to Iggy?"

"No. Does he think that too?"

"Yes, but he has nothing to back it up."

Aunt Fern walked over to the kitchen that was against the far wall. Her place was a mirror image to mine. "Tea?" she asked.

"Sure. Do you know something?"

My aunt probably didn't have any proof either, but she was a keen observer. "Many years ago, I saw those two chatting a time or two."

I laughed. "Hilary Paloma and Sheriff Duncan?"

"Yes."

"If chatting with someone meant having an affair, half the town would be called cheaters. Witch's Cove is a friendly place where neighbors help neighbors."

"You might be right, but I can read body language. They liked each other a lot," she said.

I think my aunt was looking for an excuse not to date the sheriff. "If we have any chance of proving Jaxson didn't rob the liquor store, we need to find out what happened the night of the robbery," I said.

"I didn't know you were planning something like that. It's been eleven years. And even if you do prove he was innocent, Jaxson can't get those three years back that he spent in jail."

That was the worst part. "I know, but I want to help Drake. He just got his brother back. Now Jaxson is leaving again."

"Tell me how you propose to do that? It's not like Rich's ex-wife is going to confess now. She's been remarried for years."

We talked about many options, but each one had too many loopholes.

Aunt Fern snapped her fingers. "I've got an idea."

This might be the dumbest plan ever, but if I could help Jaxson and Drake in any way, I wanted to give it a try. The next morning, Aunt Fern handed me a twenty-dollar gift card that was good for a meal at the Tiki Hut Grill that expired in three days. My goal was to convince Hilary Paloma Dinkle that she'd won this gift card. If she accepted, and if she came to the Tiki Hut, I would ambush her—I mean I would get a feel for whether she might have been with the sheriff the night of the robbery. I knew that was a tall order, but I was pretty good at getting a person to talk and then studying that person's reaction.

During the trial, I had wondered if maybe the sheriff himself had robbed the store. But when Rich Paloma described the assailant as a six-foot tall man of average build, it eliminated our sheriff—even then.

I was open to the idea that the robbery could have been committed by a totally random person. When the sheriff arrested Jaxson, he said there was no evidence of the six-pack Jaxson purchased anywhere in his house, which meant Jaxson must have tossed the beer as soon as he bought it. That seemed totally lame at the time even to my fifteen-year old self.

When Drake's dad had gone to his place to make sure the beer hadn't been overlooked, he'd found nothing either. Jaxson had claimed someone—as in the sheriff—must have confiscated it. Since Jaxson had paid cash, there was no record of him buying the beer either. I didn't know much about the law, but the case seemed circumstantial at best. I mean, the robber was wearing a mask.

Because I had spent much of last night trying to solve that cold case, the lack of sleep was playing havoc on my ability to concentrate. Thankfully, I was working on the outside patio today. While it was hot, I enjoyed the salty ocean air.

After I took a couple's order, I reentered the air-conditioned restaurant to place the order when Dolly Andrews, the owner of the Spellbound Diner, rushed in and made a beeline toward Aunt Fern who was working the cash register. Wanting front row seats for this confrontation, I hurried over to the coffee station since it placed me within hearing distance.

When these two were in the same room together, fireworks happened. Not only had Dolly and Aunt Fern fought over Harold at one time, I'd heard rumors that the two of them had actually gone out with Duncan Donut a time or two—before he was donut shaped.

"He's dead, Fern." Dolly's voice trembled.

Someone had died? My heart pounded, forcing me to move closer.

"Who's dead?" Aunt Fern asked.

"Cliff Duncan."

What? The deputy was dead? Had I been holding anything more than my order pad, I would have dropped it. Dolly had to be wrong. Not able to keep my nose out of things, I ran up to the counter. "Dolly, what are you talking about?" I asked in a loud whisper.

"Cliff is dead. I heard the sirens this morning, and of course I had to investigate. I rushed over to the sheriff's office since Pearl knows everything."

Pearl Dilsmith might be in her late seventies, and a bit absent-minded, but she was the sheriff's dispatcher, and as such, knew the comings and goings of the town better than anyone. "Good thinking. What did she say?"

"Apparently, when Cliff didn't show up to work this morning, the sheriff went looking for him. He found his son face down in the living room—dead."

My mind spun. "Was he shot?"

"I don't think so."

Okay, this was how rumors started. "Could he have died from an overdose or alcohol poisoning?" Not that I'd ever seen Cliff drunk nor had I known him to do drugs, but what other options were there? I couldn't see him having been beaten to death. Cliff was a strong, beefy man. "He couldn't have had had a heart attack, right? He was only thirty-three."

Yes, I had heard about people that young having heart failure, but it wasn't common.

"His father thinks it might have been poison. I don't know how he'd know that though," Dolly said.

I blew out a breath. The medical examiner would figure it out. Once the autopsy was performed, the body would arrive at my parents' funeral home. My mom better not ask me to work on him. That would be too much for me. Even though I worked at the Grill five days a week, I sometimes helped my parents out. Because I enjoyed doing hair and makeup, my mom often asked me to make the bodies more presentable. For the most part, I enjoyed the work.

But I had other talents beside being a makeup artist and stylist. I had my magic. Using the pink diamond from around my neck, I could often figure out how a person died—more or less accurately. Sure, a trained doctor would perform an autopsy, but not all of their results were right. Sometimes deaths could be a result of a curse, and no medical examiner would ever figure that out.

"Will his dad be investigating?" I asked. Even though he was the sheriff, it would still be a major conflict of interest. After all, his son had been murdered.

"I imagine so. Who else would do it?"

"I don't know. Maybe the mayor will bring in someone from another town." I sucked in a breath as something horrible occurred to me. "Excuse me."

I rushed down the hallway and ducked into the women's changing room to make a call in private. Drake had to be warned, or rather Jaxson had to be notified. In my heart, I believed he had nothing to do with Cliff's death, but knowing the sheriff, Jaxson would be the first one arrested. There would be no proof, of course, but when had that stopped the sheriff? He had to be reeling after finding his son dead and not thinking straight.

I called Drake.

"Glinda, I can't talk. I'm in the middle—"

I couldn't wait to hear his excuse. "Cliff Duncan is dead."

"What?"

"He's dead, and ten bucks says Sheriff Duncan will assume your brother is guilty."

He said a few unsavory words. "When did Cliff die?"

"I don't know. I didn't wait around long enough to find out all of the details."

"Jaxson took off this morning," he said.

I wasn't sure if that made him look guilty or if it would exonerate him. It all depended on when Cliff died. "Maybe you should call and warn him. He might need to return and defend himself."

Drake said nothing for a few seconds. "I know my brother. He won't go for it. They'll have to find him first."

And when the sheriff located Drake's brother, he would throw Jaxson in jail. "Maybe you're right. Now I wished Jaxson had never come back home."

"Me too."

"What we need to do is find out who killed Cliff. I'm betting there are a host of suspects. He wasn't a nice man."

"You can say that again, but you can't start asking questions. It could be dangerous."

"Don't worry. I'll be discreet."

Drake chuckled. "When have you ever been discreet?"

"Good point." If I succeeded in being circumspect, it would be the first time ever. "I have other ways of finding out things."

"Like your magic necklace?" he asked.

"Yes." The sheriff was also aware of my talent, but I don't think he believed in it. I always suspected it was because he wanted to be the hero in solving crimes. He wouldn't want some witch helping out. In this case, however, he might appreciate it.

"I guess it won't hurt to look into it, but I'm with a client. Can we meet later tonight?" Drake asked.

"Sure. Call me when you're free."

"Will do."

I didn't feel any better after telling him the bad news, but I was glad I had. He needed to know, as did Jaxson. I went back to the restaurant and glanced over at table eight, remembering how I'd just served Cliff yesterday. While I didn't like him, I didn't wish him dead either.

Everyone must have heard Dolly telling my aunt about Cliff, because for the rest of the day that was all anyone could talk about. Unfortunately, Jaxson Harrison's name was thrown out way too many times. Poor guy was guilty before anyone knew how the deputy had died.

Once three o'clock rolled around, I went upstairs to change out of my Glinda the Good Witch costume—or rather my outdoor Glinda costume. I didn't exactly remain faithful to the movie, but I wasn't about to wear a long pink dress in the hot Florida heat. No surprise, Iggy was waiting for me.

"I'm guessing you heard?" I asked the little miscreant.

"Yes. Cliff is dead! Cliff is dead!" Iggy did a little spin.

I froze. "You didn't have anything to do with his death, did you?" Other than possibly giving a person salmonella, I doubt a three-foot long iguana could kill someone.

"No, but I thank whoever did."

"Don't be like that. It's mean." Iggy scurried over to his viewing chair by the window and gave me the cold shoulder. Iggy might be close to fifteen-years old, but he was still rather immature.

I headed into my bedroom to take off my costume. While I had a closet, I used an armoire to keep my five costumes—one for each day of the week I worked. Since I sometimes worked outside, I needed to wear an outfit I wouldn't melt in. Today, I'd worn my ankle-high pink Converse sneakers, my pink shorts, and my sleeveless sequenced pink top. After I took off my bejeweled pink crown, I removed my top. I would have kept on the pink shorts if some mustard hadn't splattered on them.

Because I needed to visit my mom to see what she knew about Cliff's death, I donned my light-weight pink capri pants, along with a white top that was edged in—you guessed it—pink. I never took off my pink necklace, since my grandmother had given it to me, and I cherished it. Besides, it was imbued with my magic.

After changing, I headed over to visit my parents' funeral home. While they wouldn't be receiving Cliff's body until after the autopsy, they were plugged into the world of the dead, and I wanted to find out what they knew.

I entered through the back entrance, mostly because my mom had a thirty-foot yellow runner that went from the entrance to the chapel. Every time I walked on it, I heard the song "Follow the Yellow Brick Road" in my head.

Did I mention my mother was a total devotee of the movie *The Wizard of Oz*? She even had a Cairn Terrier that she named Toto. She spent years buying movie memorabilia and then placing it around the funeral parlor, claiming it made those grieving feel more at home. Somehow, I didn't think so.

As soon as I stepped inside, I was bombarded by the intense smell of lilies and roses, a scent I really didn't like. Mom said it was to mask any other odors that were associated with death, and she was right about that since I often worked with the incoming.

When I didn't find her in the viewing room, I went back to her office. As soon as I knocked, Toto started barking. That came as no surprise since Toto always barked. I opened the door, knelt down, and held out my hand. Looking to be petted, the Terrier rushed over, and I obliged by giving him all the attention he desired.

My mother finished doing something at her desk and then turned around. "Glinda, this is a surprise. Are you here about Cliff?"

"Yes, did you talk to him?" While she claimed she spoke to the dead, I was quite certain she was a bit clairvoyant too.

"You know it's too soon."

"With Cliff being so young, I was hoping he might be up for chatting sooner than some others. I figured it wouldn't hurt to ask."

"You're right. I did try, but he was uncommunicative."

"Did you hear how he died?" I asked.

"Why no, dear. Do you know?"

My shoulders sagged. "No, I was hoping the sheriff told you."

"Considering Cliff's age, they'll do an autopsy, which means Dr. Sanchez will need some time. I don't know if she is busy or not."

"When you get the body, will you let me do my magic on him?"

My mom stood, stepped over to me, and clasped my shoulders. "Of course, I will. You have a very special gift, and I for one don't believe you should waste it."

"Thank you."

Sometimes, the cause of death was obvious—like if the person was shot. But if it wasn't clear, that was where I came in. Don't misunderstand me. Witch's Cove is a peaceful place, but since we are a tourist destination, sometimes people get a little wild, and a few end up dead.

CHAPTER 4

Just as I walked outside to head back to my place, my cell rang. It was Penny. She'd had the day off and had probably only just heard about Cliff's death.

"Did you hear who was murdered?" she asked. I couldn't tell if she was excited or horrified.

"I did."

"Oh. Then why didn't you call and tell me?" Penny asked, sounding a bit peeved that I'd left her out of the loop.

"I'm sorry. I figured you'd be with Tommy today and wouldn't want to deal with something so upsetting. How is he feeling anyway?"

"Better. Thank you." Her tone softened. "Tell me about Cliff. I'm sure you know all of the details."

I huffed out a laugh. "Not many, unfortunately."

A car door slammed shut. "I'm dropping Tommy off at my Mom's as we speak. She just got off work. Do you want to hang out in a bit?"

That was code for gossip. "I'm meeting Drake when he's free, though three heads are better than one. How about I call you when he contacts me and the three of us can talk?"

"I'd like that." Her mom's voice sounded in the background and then little Tommy's.

I wasn't sure what Penny would be able to add, but she did have a talent that could be useful. She usually could tell if a person was lying. I would say she was better at judging a person's emotional state than being a true lie detector, but many people who knew her, paid attention to what they said in front of her. Those people would often ask: Penny for my thoughts? While clever, after a while, it became annoying.

Once inside my apartment, I glanced at the window seat, expecting to see Iggy staring longingly out the window. Only he wasn't there. "Iggy? I'm back."

No answer. Not that I minded him wandering around, but I didn't really trust him not to get into trouble. Thankfully, the only people he could communicate with were other witches. If a person didn't possess some magic, he looked like a regular pink iguana to them—not that there was anything ordinary about his pink color. While he might not be able to communicate with them, Iggy could understand what they were saying. He claimed that was what made him a great spy. Like I need another one of those!

Aunt Fern? She was the queen of spies. My aunt pretended not to hear well, but there was no truth in that. I swear her hearing was selectively excellent. People confessed things to her all the time, though that might have to do with the fact she wore her gray hair short, was a little plump, and most days came to work dressed as a fairy godmother. Her ability to effortlessly extract information from people still amazed me. I also loved the gossip she provided.

Earlier than I'd expected, Drake called. "Hi," I said as I plopped down on the sofa.

"How about coming over here now? While I won't be closing for a few hours, I'm not expecting many people on a Tuesday night."

Drake worked too much. I had suggested he adjust his hours, but the man never wanted to lose a sale. "Sure. Ah, Penny called."

"And?" he asked.

"She wants to join us." I had the sense Drake would object, so I rushed on. "She could come in handy since she is sort of a human lie detector."

"Fine."

That was easy. I jumped up. "I'll call her and head on over."

I made the call and then left a note for Iggy saying where I was and that I didn't know how long I'd be gone. My very smart familiar had taught himself to read, though if he ever learned to type and use the Internet, I'd be in real trouble.

Once I reached the back door to The Howl at the Moon Cheese and Wine Emporium, I went inside. Drake wasn't in back this time. Rather, he was in front dealing with a customer. Not wanting to have the discussion about Cliff in front of Mallory Abraham, I pretended to look around. I had to say, the vast number of cheeses did make my mouth water.

The reason I didn't want to say anything in front of Mallory was because as a cashier at the Fresh Market, she tended to listen to customer's conversation while she checked them out—and then gossip about them. The sad part was they never suspected a thing. I will admit I was a little jealous at how much she knew. Every time I approached one of my tables, they went quiet, waiting for me to ask if they needed something. I rarely learned anything juicy.

Once the gossiper left, Drake faced me. "Tell me your latest theory on who might have killed Cliff. I'm sure you have a few ideas."

I hopped up on the counter. "Do you agree that very few people liked Cliff?"

"That's a fair assumption."

"Then it could be anyone." I wasn't sure why I was being so pessimistic.

"You're no help." He tapped the counter. "Are we sure he was murdered?" Drake asked.

That was the one little sticking point. "No, but Dolly Andrews seems to think so. Don't worry, we'll learn soon enough after the autopsy, which is why we need to be ready."

Drake's brows rose. "Ready for what? Were you hired to be the new deputy?"

He was being silly. Drake totally understood that I could no more stay out of this than I could wear black. "No, but it never hurts to learn a few things that might help the sheriff find the killer. I imagine he would appreciate any clue, no matter how small."

Drake actually laughed. "I doubt that, but that won't stop you. Who is your number one suspect? And don't say my brother."

I opened my mouth. "You have to be kidding. Jaxson would not kill anyone." Okay, he had seemed a bit hot-headed when he was at the restaurant, but I couldn't really blame him. "I bet it was someone who had a beef with Cliff."

His brows rose once more. Okay, that wasn't very insightful.

"You should start with anyone he'd arrested recently. Cliff isn't, or rather wasn't, a gentle man," Drake said.

"I'll ask Pearl for a list." She was the sheriff's right-hand person.

He waved a hand. "I say go for it. Because I look out the window all too often, I'll tell you that she works until six sharp and not a minute more."

I checked my watch. It was only five now. "I still have time then. Who do you think it might have been?"

He fiddled with one of the baskets. "It could be anyone,

which is why we need more information before we start accusing people."

"I don't plan on accusing anyone," I said, though I had in the past. Hopefully, I'd learned my lesson. "Have you told your brother about Cliff's death?"

"I called him."

"Was he sad, thrilled, scared, or what?"

"Jaxson is good at hiding his emotions, especially over the phone. I'm guessing he was pleased, if that's the right word."

The front door opened, and Penny breezed in. "Sorry, I'm late. What have I missed?"

"Nothing. We haven't discussed much yet, other than there will probably be a long list of suspects," I said.

She set her purse on the counter. "No top suspect?" she asked me.

"No. We kind of thought it could be someone Cliff had recently arrested."

"I like that line of thinking, but did you know Cliff's former girlfriend is back in town?" Penny's eyebrows rose as a twinkle formed in her eyes.

I had to wrack my brain to remember who the woman was, but I came up empty. After college, I'd worked for a year, and only returned home three years ago. "No. Who was she?"

"Buffy Bigalow. Mind you, this is hearsay from a friend of my mom's, but this friend said that she is renting an apartment above the fabric store in that strip mall on the outskirts of town. She's been here about a week."

I wasn't sure why we should care if a former girlfriend had only recently arrived in town or not. "What would she have to do with Cliff's demise, especially if she just arrived?"

Penny planted a hand on her hip. "Well, she came back with a three-year old kid. You tell me."

I did the math and my mind spun. "You don't actually think it's Cliff's child, do you?"

She shrugged. Because Drake had been quiet, I glanced over at him. "What do you think?"

He held up his hands. "I don't have much experience with angry ex-girlfriends."

Or any ex-girlfriends. "Good to know," I tossed back. "Other than talking to Pearl to see what she knows about Cliff's death, I guess we'll have to wait for the medical examiner's report for cause of death."

Penny snapped her fingers. "What about Steve Rocker? He had motive."

"Who?" Drake asked.

"He's Pearl's grandson," Penny said. "I only caught a glimpse of him once or twice when he was visiting." She whistled. "Talk about tall, dark, and handsome."

Penny seemed to like all of the eligible men.

"Go on," Drake said, showing a bit of interest.

"According to Pearl, he was in the service—Marines, I think. When he got out, he majored in law enforcement at UF. I don't know why, but he came to Witch's Cove and applied for the deputy's job, even though Cliff already had the position. Steve must have thought the town was growing and needed more help. Pearl said Cliff was downright rude to him."

Penny looked rather smug about her inside knowledge. I had to admit she had a right to be. She did have two pieces of news.

"And you think because he didn't get a job that wasn't even being offered that it was motive for killing Cliff?"

She shrugged. "Just throwing out ideas."

"That's good info, but if we're going to use that logic, I should be arrested."

"Why?" Drake actually sounded concerned.

"Everyone knows I couldn't stand Cliff. He was always trying to cop a feel. The man had no manners. If homicide weren't illegal, I might have done him in myself."

That cut the tension a bit.

"Where is Steve Rocker now?" Drake asked with interest.

"Back home. I think he lives about two hours from here. Pearl said he is a security guard at some strip mall. She also said something about him not wanting to stay in his hometown for long, which was why he didn't apply for a position with the department there." Penny turned to me. "We should ask Pearl about him."

I had the sense Penny was interested in him for a date rather than as a suspect. "If you want, we can talk to her now."

Penny grinned. "I'm game."

Since Drake needed to stay at the store in case anyone stopped by, the two of us left.

Penny grabbed my arm. "We should take something to her—to soften her up. Pearl loves cookies," Penny said.

"How do you know that?"

Penny stopped before crossing the street. "Let's just say Sam has had a few run-ins with Cliff and has spent some time in jail. Mind you, one or two of those times were because I turned in the deadbeat for failing to pay child support."

"I remember you telling me that." That might be one reason why I was single and planned to stay that way. "Good idea about the cookies. I'm sure Aunt Fern won't mind donating to the cause."

We went in through the Tiki Hut's front door. Aunt Fern was chatting with someone at a table, so Penny and I were able to slip into the kitchen without notice. Since To-Go bags were stacked on the counter, I grabbed one and dropped in an assortment of goodies for Pearl.

Not wanting to chance my aunt stopping us on our way out, we exited the back way. After walking around the northside of the building, we cut across the large parking lot before crossing the street.

Pearl was at her desk shuffling some papers, but I couldn't tell if she was really busy or just pretending to be. She looked up and gave us a sad smile. Maybe she really had liked Cliff.

"Pearl, I'm sorry for your loss. We brought you some cookies to cheer you up."

"What loss? That no good deputy caused more harm than good, if you ask me."

Aha! A woman after my own heart. Both Penny and I stepped closer. "What do you know?"

"The sheriff is out searching for the killer now."

"So Cliff was murdered?" I asked.

"The sheriff seems to think so." I waited for Pearl to offer a list of her suspects, but she was too busy opening the bag of cookies and sniffing them. She grinned and then stuffed one in her mouth. Once she finished the first one, she plucked another from the bag. "These are really good," she said.

"Our chef is very talented." Clearly, I needed to be a bit more aggressive about extracting information. "Who do you think killed Cliff?"

At the moment, nobody was in either of the two holding cells to overhear our conversation. "That's hard to say."

Darn. "Who did Cliff recently arrest or at least bring in for questioning? They might have wanted to harm him."

"Let me see." She pulled open her top desk drawer and extracted a piece of paper. I was a bit surprised that she hadn't entered the information into the computer. "How far back do you want me to go?"

There couldn't be that many arrests. Witch's Cove was a relatively peaceful town. "I don't know. A month or two?"

Pearl looked up at Penny. "Your ex was in here once or twice, but you already knew that."

"Yes," Penny said. "Who else? Someone who might have been angry at Cliff for catching him."

"There were two teens Cliff caught drinking in the park one night, but their parents bailed them out before the night was through."

Maybe this was a bad idea. "What about Buffy Bigalow?"

Pearl froze. "What about her?"

I glanced over at Penny. We'd hit pay dirt.

CHAPTER 5

I had planned to pursue Hilary Paloma Dinkle and her connection to Sheriff Duncan, but Cliff's death had to take precedence. Once Cliff's murderer was brought to justice, I'd see about clearing Jaxson's name, though the time he'd spent in prison could never be recouped.

After thanking Pearl for her information, I had to contain my excitement at this potential lead. Once outside, we moved away from the window so Pearl couldn't see us.

Penny grinned. "I say we visit Buffy."

"Agreed, but you aren't thinking she might have killed Cliff, are you? I mean Cliff was a six-foot tall man with a fair amount of muscles."

"No, but she might know something," Penny said.

"I hope so, but she's only been in town a few days. Pearl said she moved away a little more than three years ago."

Penny smiled again. "Which means Cliff could be the dad. I wonder if he told her to get out of town back then?"

"It's possible Buffy left on her own accord, and Cliff never knew he was going to be a father. Maybe she came back because she wanted child support." A number of additional scenarios ran through my mind. "But we won't find out standing here, now will we?"

We rushed across the street to the parking lot.

"We can take my car," Penny said.

"Good. My car keys are in my apartment."

The trip to the south end of town took less than eight minutes. Once there, Penny parked. "What are you going to say to her, other than offering our condolences?" I asked Penny. "I don't think we can come out and ask if Cliff is the dad." Even I knew that would be tacky.

She shot me a rather frightened look. "What am *I* going to say? You always do the talking."

"You found her."

Before we could decide anything, we were at her front door. Penny knocked and then a child cried inside. A moment later, a blonde woman answered the door with a small boy behind her, clinging to her leg, his eyes as wide as saucers. "May I help you?" the woman asked.

Okay, this was awkward. I might have just said I was sorry for her loss and left if the woman's cheek hadn't been purple and a bit swollen. My thoughts went in a thousand directions. "Buffy Bigalow?" I asked, hoping I didn't mess this up.

"Yes."

"I'm Glinda Goodall. We're here about Cliff Duncan."

Her eyes narrowed, and then her hand rubbed her cheek. "I don't ever want to hear his name again."

O-kay. "Did he do that to you?" I nodded to her face.

She opened the door wide. "Yes, but I don't need everyone to hear. Come in."

I did a mental fist pump. "Thank you."

Buffy was really pretty, with long, bleached blonde hair pulled back with a hair tie. She motioned us to sit on the sofa. The rental was standard Florida beach fare with a rattan sofa covered in flowered fabric and photos of seagulls and sunsets on the walls.

After picking up her son, she sat across from us. "Did Cliff send you?"

I guess she hadn't heard. "No. He was murdered this morning." Or maybe he was murdered last night. I really didn't know.

Her breath caught, and then her gaze shot around the room as she let out a big breath. "Cliff is dead?"

She certainly sounded convincing that she was unaware he'd died. I could only hope Penny would confirm or deny it afterward. "Yes."

"How?"

"I don't know. It's too soon to tell."

Buffy held her son closer. "I guess you heard we'd dated."

"We did."

Penny smiled down at the towhead. "Your little boy is adorable. He looks a lot like my son."

Buffy stroked her son's hair. "Dusty is my everything."

Aw. "You said Cliff roughed you up. Why?"

A tear trickled down her cheek. "Cliff is Dusty's dad." She huffed. "We dated for maybe six months when I found out I was pregnant. As soon as I told him, he demanded that I leave town since it wouldn't look good for a law enforcement agent to have a child out of wedlock." She rolled her eyes.

Ouch. That wasn't nice, though I wasn't surprised by his archaic views. It was always possible he feared what his old-fashioned dad would say.

"Did you want to get married or something?" I had to ask.

"No! Cliff and I liked to party together, but that was all."

That wasn't all, but I kept my mouth shut for a change. "If you left, why did you come back?"

Dusty started to fuss, and she picked up a stuffed dinosaur off the coffee table and handed it to him. He quieted. "I left here and moved to Morganville, because I had a friend there. That was where I met Greg. He was kind and wonderful. He loved Dusty, so we moved in together about a year ago. Life was really good until he lost his job." She shook her head. "He changed on a dime and kind of took it out on me. For Dusty's sake, I had to get out."

I wanted to grab her hand, but I doubted she wanted my sympathy. "I totally understand. Were you the one who got in touch with Cliff when you returned to Witch's Cove?"

"No! Cliff found me. I had forgotten what a small town this place is. When he saw Dusty, he suddenly decided that he wanted visitation rights, but there was no way I was going to give him my child. Three years is a long time. I didn't know what kind of man Cliff had become. Not only that, going to court would cost a lot of money—money I don't have."

"So, you didn't come back here with the intent of getting back together with Cliff?"

"No. My parents live here." She shook her head. "We never had a great relationship before I had a child. I was hoping to change that. I was lucky to convince the owner of this apartment to give me a month-to-month lease. After Cliff found me and did this to me, I knew I had to leave. Again."

She should have pressed charges against him for assault, though who knows if it would have stuck. His father was the sheriff after all. "That's smart, but I guess unnecessary now." As much as I believed her, something seemed off. "I take it Greg was okay that you just left?"

The unbruised portion of her face turned pinker than Iggy's skin. "No. He won't stop calling."

"Does he want you to return?" Most men who abused women needed to have them around.

"Yes, but I don't think he's interested in me as much as Dusty. He loves my son."

That was kind of sad. "Did Greg know that Dusty's father lives in Witch's Cove."

"Yes." Her son started to cry, and Buffy looked as if she was about to crumble.

"If you need any help or just want to talk, I'll be at the Tiki Hut Grill," I said. "I work there until three most days."

"I know the place. Thank you."

Poor Buffy. She had to process her baby daddy being dead, as well as trying to heal. I wouldn't wish that on anyone.

As soon as we made it back to the car, I turned to Penny. "What do you think?"

"I think she was telling the truth."

"Good to know."

We drove back to the parking lot next to the Tiki Hut. "Thanks for letting me join you and Drake today," Penny said.

"Are you kidding? We never would have known about Buffy without you."

"It didn't help much, other than learning what we already knew—that Cliff wasn't a nice person. I'm just glad he never was interested in me," Penny said.

"You're right about that." I pushed open the car door. "See you tomorrow then."

"Yup. Have a good night."

Once Penny drove off, I called Drake and filled him in.

"What is your take on everything?" he asked.

"I don't think Steve Rocker is a suspect, and Buffy seems to be a victim."

"Back to square one then?" he asked.

"Yes, but the autopsy should be finished soon. Maybe that will help."

"Let me know," he said, sounding a bit despondent.

"Are you okay?"

"Yeah. I'm just worried about Jaxson."

"Me too."

I took the walkway that cut between the Tiki Hut and my parents' mortuary and entered through the side door that led to the restaurant's storage room. Sometimes, I wasn't in the mood to go through the gift shop or the front entrance. Clara, the woman who worked in the gift shop, could be a bit chatty.

Upstairs, I was happy to see Iggy sitting on his stool looking out. He spun around and lifted up a small branch covered in Oleander flowers. He hopped down and handed it to me. "This is for you."

"Thank you. These are lovely, but you do know they are poisonous?"

"Yes, but I didn't think you ate flowers."

"I don't." I took his offering and went into the kitchen. From the cabinet, I pulled out a small vase, filled it with water, and placed the branch in it. "Why give me a gift?"

"I should have told you I would be out and about, and I forgot to mention it."

Were the flowers an apology? If so, I'd take it. "I wasn't worried. I assumed you could take care of yourself." If anything happened to him though, I don't know what I'd do.

"So, tell me what you and Drake figured out."

Ah, so the flower was more of a bribe. I debated withholding information, but Iggy would badger me until I told him, so I gave him the run down.

"No, suspects then?" He whipped his tail back and forth.

"None I'm convinced is the killer. What did you find out?"

"Same as you. No one liked our deputy, but the only name I heard was Jaxson's."

That was what I was afraid of. "Have you eaten today?" I asked him, not in the mood to discuss this anymore.

"I did. The sea oats are quite tasty this time of year—as are the hibiscus flowers."

From the refrigerator, I pulled out a bag of fresh spinach, along with some kale and placed a few leaves of each on a plate. "If you get hungry."

"Thanks."

Just as I was about to throw something in the microwave for myself, my cell rang. It was probably Penny with more ideas. When I looked at the caller I.D., I tensed. It was Drake and we'd just hung up. "Hey, is something wrong?"

"Yes, the sheriff hunted down Jaxson and arrested him."

The air shot out of my lungs. "He can't do that. On what grounds?"

Drake barked out a laugh. "On the grounds that he's Jaxson Harrison—ex con."

I didn't want to believe the sheriff could be so prejudiced. Or maybe he could be. "I thought Jaxson wasn't in town when Cliff died."

"Apparently, Cliff died before Jaxson left."

That wasn't good. "Surely the sheriff had other evidence."

"The sheriff wouldn't tell me if he did. It's possible some neighbor thought they saw Jaxson snooping around Cliff's house the night he died. It's all I can think of that would be enough to take him in."

"What can I do?"

"Nothing for now. I tried to talk to my brother, but the sheriff said that Jaxson doesn't have visiting rights yet."

"That's bogus. Dunkin Donut shouldn't even be investigating his son's case. I can't believe the mayor didn't ask someone from another town to investigate."

"I know. Let's hope he's trying to find someone. Even if he is, I imagine it will take a few days to free up someone."

"Maybe." Poor Drake. He sounded so sad. "I'll talk to Aunt Fern. She seems to have some pull with our illustrious sheriff."

"I appreciate it. Let me know if you learn anything."

"I will," I said.

I disconnected and found Iggy on top of the kitchen counter, munching on the plate of greens. So much for the filling sea oats and wonderful hibiscus flowers. He looked up. "What?"

"Nothing. Jaxson was arrested."

"He didn't do it," Iggy said with a lot of conviction.

"Tell me what you know."

CHAPTER 6

Iggy hopped down from the kitchen counter and returned to his perch. Without answering my question about what he had learned on Cliff's demise, he merely looked out at the now mostly darkened skies.

I stepped behind him. What light there was came from the moon and string lights surrounding the Tiki Hut below. The citronella candles were glowing, and about half the seats were occupied. It looked so inviting that I decided to go downstairs for a strong drink. I needed one. But first, I wanted to hear what Iggy had to say, and then I had to eat.

"Spill."

He turned around and then lifted his chest like he always did when he thought he was superior to us mere mortals. "Penny's ex had a run in with Cliff a few weeks ago."

"I already know that."

His chest lowered a bit. "But did you know Sam punched Cliff?"

"No." I hadn't realized Penny's ex was violent. "I'll ask her about it. Anything else?"

"No, but I think there are people out there who know the truth. You just need to find them."

"We could say that about most crimes," I offered.

"All I'm saying is don't take everything you hear at face value." He turned around and returned to watching the moonbeams bounce off the shimmering ocean.

Too tired to think about his comment, I heated up a meal that the Tiki Hut chef had given me. I ate most of it, all the while wracking my brain about who could have wanted Cliff dead. Killing was a far cry from just not liking the guy.

A nice Chunky Monkey cocktail was just the thing to bring forth my creative juices. I didn't need the rum as much as I wanted the delicious banana liqueur and the chocolate topping with coconut sprinkles. That should stimulate my mind—or so I wanted to believe.

I grabbed my credit card and phone and stuffed them in my pocket. "Don't wait up for me," I told Iggy.

"Don't worry about me."

I didn't ask what that meant either. Downstairs, I found a seat at the Tiki Hut next to Chas Williams. The air was a bit muggy, but the temperature was almost pleasant. While I didn't know Chas well, I'd seen him with Cliff a few times.

"Hi, Chas," I said as I slipped onto the seat next to him.

His eyes narrowed. "I've seen you around here."

"I am usually the one wearing a pink, jeweled tiara."

His eyes brightened in recognition and then dimmed just as fast. "Oh, yes. You're a waitress here."

He said that with too much disdain. And who was he? The Sultan of Brunei or something? I really disliked people who put down other people's professions. "I am. Name's Glinda by the way."

"As in the Good Witch of the South?"

Like I hadn't heard that joke my whole life. "The one and

only." Even though I'd come here for a drink, I didn't want to squander the opportunity to learn something. As Iggy said, someone knew what really happened to creepy Cliff. "It's sad about Cliff, isn't it?"

I was so going to burn for lying.

"It is. And to think he'd just found out he was a dad."

While I've never taken any acting classes, I was quite proud that I was able to control my emotions, especially when I knew the truth—assuming Buffy could be believed. "Cliff, a dad? That's wonderful and tragic at the same time. Who's the mom?" As if I didn't know.

"Someone he met about four years ago. Her name is Buffy Bigalow."

"I thought I heard she moved away right before I returned home three years ago." I was good.

"That's about right."

Chas tossed back his drink and set the bottle down, looking as if he was going to leave, and I couldn't let that happen. I needed him to tell me what he knew about who might have killed Cliff. I waved to Nick, who was working the bar tonight. Since May was hot this time of year, Nick was dressed as Tarzan. Seeing how most of the clientele were women, I assumed they came for the nice view.

"Can I get a Chunky Monkey?" I asked Nick. I then turned to Chas. "Can I buy you another drink?"

I was certain lightning would strike me dead for offering to buy this guy a beer, but I needed information.

"Sure."

"Another for Chas." I turned back to my seat mate. I hoped he might have learned something from the sheriff since he and Cliff appeared to be tight. "Did you hear how Cliff died?"

"No, you?"

"No." I blew out an exaggerated breath. "Any idea who might have done this? I can understand a man of the law dying in some shootout during a crime, but to be killed in his own house is downright scary."

"I totally agree. Cliff was a strong man, so it would have taken a lot to bring him down. I spoke with the sheriff, and he said he didn't find any defensive wounds or see any obvious injuries."

That was good intel. "Interesting. I suppose Cliff could have been shot with a tranquilizer and then…" I couldn't even finish the sentence, not wanting to think about what might come next. Where that idea had come from, I don't know. I wasn't psychic or anything.

Chas chuckled. "You've seen one too many television crime shows."

No, I'm a witch and know a thing or two about death. "Maybe."

Nick delivered Chas' beer who then took a long gulp before setting down his drink. "Do you have any theories?" he asked.

"No. I actually came here tonight for a drink, hoping to gain some clarity about the problem. All I keep thinking is that maybe some witch put a spell on him to make his heart stop."

"A witch could stop a heart?" Chas laughed.

Note to self: Not everyone in this town was a believer. "As I said, it's just a theory. What do you think happened? Without any defensive wounds or obvious cause of death, it kind of narrows it down."

"I don't think it was a heart attack. In high school, Cliff was a big jock, and he more or less kept himself in shape ever since. I'm almost leaning toward your tranquilizer theory."

"I made that up." Even if it were true, I didn't know what the killer would do after Cliff was comatose on the floor—

inject him with a lethal dose of insulin or poison maybe? "I honestly didn't know Cliff all that well. I mostly saw him when he came in for lunch or dinner. Did he do drugs by any chance?" If he had overdosed, the medical examiner would be able to tell.

"Cliff? Nothing strong enough to kill him."

That was interesting. "You said he just found out he was a dad. Was he happy about it?"

Not that I thought Buffy would lie—mostly because Penny said she was telling the truth—but no witch was infallible.

"Very much so. Just goes to show you how people can change. A few years ago, getting married and having a family was the last thing on his mind. I don't know what happened, but he seemed to have had a change of heart. Maybe it was because Buffy dumped him. You know the saying: You want what you can't have."

Was that really a saying or just an idea? It didn't matter. Buffy had claimed Cliff told her to get out of town, not the other way around. Someone wasn't being honest.

Chas ran his thumb nail down the bottle to scrape off the label. I wanted to know more, but I wasn't sure what to ask him.

Cliff's friend sat up straighter, faced me, and held up his beer in a toast. "To Cliff."

I swallowed hard and tapped my glass to his. "To Cliff."

After I finished my delicious drink, I gave my sympathies to Chas once more. He really did seem to have been Cliff's friend, even though it was clear Cliff had never confided in him about knowing Buffy had been pregnant three and a half years ago. I finished my drink, paid my bill, and then slipped off the stool.

"Night, Chas."

"Goodnight, Glinda."

I was tempted to scribble my email address on a napkin and ask him to let me know if he heard anything about Cliff's death, but he probably already thought I was just a nosy busybody, and he'd be mostly right.

Needing a hot shower and some sleep, I headed upstairs to bed.

The next morning after I dressed, I went downstairs into work. I usually had today off, but Corinne, another one of the servers wanted to switch days. I didn't mind, especially since the middle of the week wasn't very busy.

I was feeling okay about the progress I'd made on Cliff's murder until a couple from Georgia told me they had their hotel room robbed last night while they were out and about. The last thing Witch's Cove needed was bad press.

"Did you call the cops?" I asked them. Shoot. I'd forgotten for a moment the sheriff was the only one left.

The husband sat up straighter. "We sure did, but he said he found nothing to indicate who might have broken in. It's not like we could ask him to process all of the fingerprints in the room."

The wife scrunched up her face and shook her head, but I didn't want to know what she'd been thinking. "That could take a long time for sure," I said.

"The sheriff told us his son had just died, and we really didn't want to be a burden."

How sweet was that. "Yes. The whole town is still reeling over the deputy's death. What was stolen from your room?"

The couple exchanged glances. "I stupidly left my purse in one of the drawers," the wife said. "All my money and credit cards were taken. I called the bank to stop any charges, but I had a good amount of cash. We'll live, but I feel so violated."

"I am so sorry." My heart broke for them. Needless to say, I doubted this couple would return to Witch's Cove any time soon. "Did you look in the dumpster to see if maybe they took the cash and tossed the purse?" As I've said, I can't stop trying to solve problems.

"The sheriff did, and he found my wife's purse, but it was empty."

"We don't hold a grudge against whoever it was. If the thief was that desperate to steal, then maybe we helped him in some small way."

Wow. I don't think I'd have such a good attitude. "Maybe you did. What else is the sheriff going to do to find this guy?"

"He already asked several other motel guests if they saw anyone skulking about last night, and all anyone heard were howling noises out back in the woods."

"Wolves maybe?"

"Or some wild dogs," he said.

There was nothing else I could add, and I didn't want to take up any more of their time. "I hope the rest of your stay goes better." I wasn't good at offering sympathy despite my father being amazing at it.

When I told Aunt Fern about what happened to the couple, she said she'd give them a steep discount on their meal. My aunt was the best.

Once the couple left, the remainder of my morning was business as usual until a tour bus arrived, and then serving everyone became chaotic. Me, Penny, and Ray—another server who usually worked outside—abandoned our assigned tables and served whoever needed the help. By two, I was totally beat.

As suddenly as the crowd came, they left, giving me a chance to catch my breath before my shift ended. I spotted

Penny delivering food to the one remaining table when her phone rang. Because she was carrying a rather large tray, I rushed over to help her. "I'll take that. Get your call. It could be about Tommy."

Her faced paled. "Thank you."

Once we made the transfer, she snatched her cell out of her pocket and answered it. "What is it, Sam?" she asked, sounding rather annoyed.

As Penny moved to the quieter hallway in front of the kitchen, I delivered the food to her table. After I asked if they needed anything else, I went to check on my friend. Considering how she disliked talking to her ex for longer than necessary, I was surprised she was still on the phone with him. Eventually, she ended the call, not looking happy at all.

"Is everything okay?" I asked.

"That was Sam. He said that when he came home for lunch, his front door was ajar."

I needed a moment to process the information. "Was he robbed?" I shivered at the thought of there being a thief on the loose. Two robberies in one day would be highly unusual.

"No, that's the thing. Nothing was disturbed."

I sighed. "He probably thought he'd locked the door, and the wind blew it open or something."

"That's what I told him, but he is certain someone entered his house."

"If nothing was disturbed, how could he tell? Did it smell different?"

"I don't know. He's adamant that someone had been there though."

I wasn't buying it. "Did he call the sheriff?"

Penny tilted her head to the side. "And say what?"

"I don't know. I guess not much if he didn't really have anything to report." I blew out a breath. "One good thing was that at least he didn't have Tommy today. Sam might have interrupted a robbery in progress."

Penny palmed her chest. "That would have been horrible."

"No kidding." A woman sat down at one of my tables, and I nodded in her direction. "I have to wait on her."

"Go," Penny said.

I'd just taken the customer's order and delivered the ticket to the kitchen when my cell rang. It was my mom.

"Hey, what's up?" I asked.

"I know you're at work, but I thought you should know that the medical examiner finished her autopsy. Cliff died of natural causes."

That was not what I expected her to say. "For real? Are you buying that?"

"Not in the least. I've been trying to contact Cliff ever since the report, but something is blocking me."

"Does that mean you think a witch is involved?" I asked, keeping my voice low. While I've never heard of one of our witches stopping a person's heart, it was possible, especially since we weren't the only town around here that had witches.

"I have no idea," my mom said. "That's why I'd like you to come over."

"I can't leave work. I don't get off for another hour. I'll stop over then."

"Fine." Mom disconnected, not sounding all that pleased. Sheesh.

I headed back to my table to check on my customer. After refreshing the lady's coffee, I returned the pot to the table that was against the side wall.

Penny rushed over to me. "Who was on the phone? Was it Drake? Did he learn anything?"

Penny's words came out so fast, my head almost spun. Why would Drake know anything about Sam and his possible break-in? Or did she think Drake would be investigating Cliff's death? "No, it was my mom. The medical examiner finished the autopsy."

"And?"

I clutched Penny's arm and escorted her to the back hallway. I didn't need those in the restaurant to hear—especially Aunt Fern. She'd just blab it to everyone who came up to cash out.

"He died of natural causes."

Penny shook her head so hard the pennies on her skirt jangled. "Do you believe that?"

"No, which is why I will be using this." I lifted my pink diamond pendant—okay, my fake pink diamond pendant—off my neck and swung it back and forth.

"You'll learn the truth," Penny said with a lot of confidence.

"Let's hope so, for the sheriff's sake and for Jaxson's."

"Jaxson?" Penny asked.

I knew it. She still had a crush on him even after all these years. "The sheriff arrested him yesterday evening."

Penny's mouth opened. "On what evidence?"

She was wonderfully naïve. "I doubt the sheriff had any."

"Then we have to find out who really killed Cliff."

She wasn't listening. "It's all good. Cliff died of natural causes. Duncan Donut will have to let Jaxson go since he son wasn't murdered."

Her eyes widened. "That's right. Cliff wasn't murdered—or so the medical examiner claimed."

"Bingo."

Penny sighed. "Do you think Jaxson will stay in town now?"

Really? "No. It will be all the more reason for him to leave."

Her shoulders slumped. "That's too bad."

"I know."

Penny tapped my pink stone. "What if you find out Cliff was murdered?"

My heart nearly stopped. "For both Drake and Jaxson's sake, I hope I don't."

CHAPTER 7

As soon as I clocked out, I changed and then headed out. Before I used my magical abilities on Cliff's corpse, I had to talk to Drake. Did he even know that Cliff had died of natural causes? He'd want to know that his brother would be set free.

I rushed past the funeral home to the wine shop and yanked on the back door. It was locked. That was odd. Even though Tuesdays and Wednesdays were Drake's slow days, which meant he opened at two instead of at ten a.m., he should be there. All I could think of was that the sheriff had already released Jaxson, and Drake and his brother were celebrating somewhere. If that were the case, Drake should have put a sign on the door to let his customers know the store was closed.

Drake probably left a note on the front door since hardly anyone entered by the beach entrance. If he and Jaxson were celebrating, could they be at the Tiki Hut? Since I hadn't even looked in that direction when I left, I turned around and hiked back to our outside bar.

Only three people in bathing suits were seated, but Drake

and Jaxson were nowhere to be found. My feelings were hurt a bit, but in all honesty, it wasn't as if we were the only drinking establishment in town.

Since my mom was expecting me, I couldn't waste time looking for these two happy campers. After avoiding the inevitable for long enough, I returned to the funeral home. As soon as I unlocked the back door and stepped inside, I sensed a presence. Could it be Cliff's spirit? That was more my mom's forte, but I did have other talents beside being able to identify how a person died.

My initial plan had been to check his body and leave. With this new spirit swirling about, however, I thought I should talk to Mom first. Instead of being in her office, she was in the conference room, one that was reserved for when my parents met with families of the deceased. As soon as I walked in, she held up a hand as if to say I shouldn't disturb her, and I immediately stopped moving.

The lack of overhead lights, the lit candles placed in a circle, along with the sprinkling of sage indicated my mom was trying to contact Cliff. She closed her eyes and then began to chant softly. It was like a one-person seance. As much as I thought I could help by adding my energy, I remained where I was.

After a few minutes, she lowered her head and then straightened. She looked up and smiled. "Come in, dear."

I took a seat across from her. "What did Cliff say?"

While I couldn't be positive that was who she was communicating with, it was a good guess.

She shook her head. "I don't think I've ever met a more clueless man."

That didn't sound good. "What do you mean?"

"I asked him how he passed, and all he could recall was that he was in his backyard one minute, and the next he felt a little sting near the top of his spine."

"Like a mosquito bite or a needle?"

"He thought he'd been bitten by a bug or maybe a spider. When his skin started to burn, he went inside. The next thing he knew, he was being welcomed by some out-of-body entity. He felt warmth, love, and contentment for the first time in his life. True peace, he called it."

My idea of a tranquilizer gun might not have been that far off, but he would have woken up at some point—unless he had been poisoned with something that was rather fast acting. "He didn't say if he saw anyone?"

"I asked him that. He said he didn't."

"Did he have any concept of time passing?"

"That's the strange part," my mother said. "He couldn't say how long it was between the sting and his death. As I said: clueless. I figure if he didn't show up for work this morning, it could have been as long as sixteen hours or as few as one. I should have asked Dr. Sanchez when he died. That would be something important to know."

"I agree." I clasped my pink diamond pendant. "I'll see if his body will be more forthcoming than clueless Cliff."

"Thank you, dear. He's on tray four."

Tray four. Could that be any more antiseptic? It would have been nice if my parents had given the coolers better names, like Sweet Dreams, At Peace, Conflict Begone, and Heaven Sent. Even if I suggested it, they'd never change it. They have always been rather entrenched in their ways.

I went back down the hall to the morgue, located Cliff's body, and slid him onto the prep table. I liked to do my magic while the body was out of the cooler since I had the sense that the refrigeration might affect my abilities. Not that the room was warm in any way, but it was better than him being on the slab itself.

After I removed my necklace and centered myself, I focused on what I needed to do and not on the fact that someone I'd interacted with almost every day lay before me. Having grown up around death, I should be immune to it, but I wasn't.

It was time to begin. Starting at Cliff's feet and moving upward, I used slow, circular movements with my pink pendant. With each rotation, I watched for the light pink stone to change color. Not that my magic was foolproof mind you—don't forget how my spell to get my familiar had gone very wrong—but I had more hits than misses. From past experience, I usually didn't pick up much until I was closer to the heart. Working hard to keep my movements smooth, I moved up the body, expecting to see the stone turn green any moment. Green implied a blockage of some kind. In most cases, that signaled a heart attack, which would be deemed a natural cause.

As I approached his stomach though, I thought I saw the stone flicker purple, meaning a poison was present, but when I swept it across his body a second time, it was pink again. My imagination must be going crazy. As much as I wanted to stop, I couldn't. Too much was riding on this outcome.

I was almost to his chin when the stone shimmered purple again. My pulse soared and my hand shook. "Keep it nice and steady," I told myself.

Needing to be thorough, I moved the stone to the top of his head, and the stone paled once more. When my arm spasmed from the tension, I lowered it. I needed a moment to calm myself before I repeated the process. Only then would I ask for my mother's help. She would tell me if my eyes were playing tricks on me.

I understood what my findings would do to Drake and his brother if I concluded that Cliff hadn't died from natural causes. It could destroy my relationship with my best male friend and put Jaxson through another trial. While that would be beyond terrible, I could never lie about my findings. If I did, it would eat away at me for life.

Taking even more care the second time, I swept the body again, but the results remained the same. My stomach churned. Cliff had been poisoned. Why hadn't Dr. Sanchez picked up on that? Sure, there were about five thousand poisons, and as such would have been impossible to test for all of them, but shouldn't there have been something in his stomach to indicate it? I had no medical training, so perhaps Cliff had lived long enough to metabolize what he'd ingested.

If only my stone exhibited more than just one shade of purple, I might have been able to tell exactly what had killed him. I would then have looked up the symptoms. Was it an untraceable poison? Could it have left the body within a few hours? I could only hope the good Dr. Sanchez—or the center for poison control—would have the answers.

I placed my necklace around my neck and went in search of my mother since I still wanted her opinion. This time I found her in her office, and when I stepped inside, Toto barked as usual. After I gave him the required number of rubs, he settled down.

"What did you find?" she asked.

I told her. "Do you have a minute? I would like a second set of eyes."

She pushed back her chair. "Of course."

"Where's Dad? I didn't see him anywhere." In fact, I hadn't seen him the last few times I was here.

"He's feeling a little under the weather."

Oh no. "What's wrong?"

"It's nothing, dear. Each death takes a lot out of your father. He just needs his rest."

I'd heard that before. Dealing with grief wasn't easy on the spirit. Lucky for my mom, she didn't have to deal with the families nearly as much. She did most of the paperwork at the funeral home, sending out the bills, arranging for the viewings, and coordinating the burials.

I followed her to the morgue. Thankfully, Cliff hadn't moved. Yes, I know he was dead, but I somehow expected him to sit up at any moment and say it was all a joke. That would be so like him.

Okay, I was losing my mind. I needed to focus.

After I removed my necklace once more, I repeated the slow scan, going once more from toe to head.

"There!" my mother exclaimed as the pendant passed over his stomach. I stopped for a moment. "That's odd. It's gone now," she said.

"The same thing happened to me. Just wait. It will glow again."

When I ran the stone over his heart, it slightly changed color. As I moved higher, the purple intensified, being the strongest around his neck area.

"What do you think?" I asked my mom.

"The purple implies poison, but the lack of it in his stomach is perplexing. We need to ask Elissa about it."

Elissa was Dr. Sanchez, the medical examiner. "I will definitely be asking her a few questions." As in right now.

"I'll put the body back," Mom said. "You go do your thing, but don't be a stranger."

"I won't." I hugged my mother. "Thanks again."

As soon as I stepped outside into the hot and muggy air, I inhaled deeply to get the scent of death out of my lungs. I had a lot to contemplate. I needed to speak with Dr. Sanchez, but first, I had to shower. Death wasn't a good perfume.

In the apartment, Iggy raced up to me. "You look like you know something."

He scooted out of the way so I wouldn't step on him. "I haven't said a word."

"There is a vibe of despair radiating off you."

Where did my animal come up with this stuff? Since I needed to tell someone, and he was here, I decided to give him a rundown. "But first, you have to promise not to say a word."

He swished his light and dark striped pink tail. "My lips are sealed."

"When have they ever been sealed?"

"Fine, don't tell me."

Iggy knew that kind of challenge would get me to talk fast. "Okay. Cliff was poisoned."

"I knew it!" he said with too much enthusiasm.

"Excuse me. How could you know? You would have told me if you knew."

His mouth opened and then closed. "Did I or did I not bring you an Oleander flower?"

"Yes, but what does that have to do with anything?" Then it dawned on me. "Are you saying Cliff was poisoned with Oleander?"

"I can't say for sure, but there must have been some reason why I picked it. Call it my intuition or my stellar psychic abilities."

Psychic abilities, indeed. "I'm taking a shower. When I finish, I want some answers. Real ones."

"Fine." With his head held high, he rushed over to his stool, hopped up on it, and looked out the window. It was a beautiful day with vast amounts of white, fluffy sand greeting the Gulf of Mexico. I really wished I had the time to relax on a lounge chair on the beach and smell that sea air—but I didn't. I had to talk to Dr. Sanchez.

Once I finished removing the stench from my body, I tossed my clothes in the hamper. How my mother stayed in the morgue all day long and not feel grungy, I'd never understand.

I threw on my pink jeans—the ones with the pretty pink

lace insets—and a dark pink top. Instead of sneakers, I slipped on a pair of pink sandals since it was dreadfully hot out today.

When I returned to the living room, Iggy was on the kitchen counter munching on lettuce that I didn't remember taking out of the refrigerator—or was I really losing it? It was always possible he'd gone downstairs and stolen some from the kitchen. I wouldn't put it past him.

"What did you figure out?" I asked Iggy.

"About what?"

Now he was being coy? "About Cliff's death."

"I told you what I know," he shot back. "It's you who needs to talk to the experts to learn more."

Hadn't I already told him that was my plan. Darn. I couldn't remember. "That is what I'm about to do." The last time I challenged Dr. Sanchez's findings though, she was not happy. When other evidence came into play that proved I was right, she gave me some respect. This time I wanted to do things differently. "Wish me luck."

"You don't need it. You have me."

I turned my back and rolled my eyes. Iggy, Iggy, Iggy.

CHAPTER 8

I knocked on Dr. Sanchez's office door.
"Come in."
I bet she didn't get many visitors other than the sheriff and Cliff, though from now on, she'd only interact with the sheriff.

I stepped inside. "Hi, Dr. Sanchez. Do you have a minute?"

"Sure. Did your mother need something?"

"Not exactly." To quell my nerves, I fiddled with my necklace, but even touching my magic stone didn't help calm me.

The medical examiner's eyes widened. "Don't tell me you have a theory about the cause of Cliff's death?"

Don't tell her? I had to. And it wasn't a theory. "What can you tell me about Oleander poisoning?"

She let out a breath, lifted her reading glasses, and placed them on top of her head. "It depends on how much was ingested. A lot and it could kill the person right away, but if the person only had a little, it would cause his heart to slow or give him an irregular heartbeat. This person would have blurred vision, a loss of appetite, and be confused, along with a host of other symptoms. Why? Did your iguana eat some leaves?"

"No, he's a bit smarter than that. On a slightly different note, before Cliff died, he told my mom that he felt a sting at the back of his neck."

Dr. Sanchez tilted her chin downward. "Excuse me? Your mother spoke with Cliff before he died? Why didn't she call 911?"

This wasn't going as I'd hoped. "I thought you knew that my mother can speak with the dead."

"No, I didn't know," she said with quite a lot of doubt in her voice.

I realized the good doctor was new to Witch's Cove, but gossip about who was who in town usually traveled a lot faster. "She can."

Dr. Sanchez seemed to ponder that for a moment and then looked up at me. "And what else did Cliff tell her?" She motioned I take the only remaining seat in her office.

I sat and then told her what my mom had said. "Cliff seemed a bit confused, which fits with the symptoms you mentioned."

She nodded, but I didn't get the sense she was buying any of it. "How did you decide Cliff was poisoned with Oleander?"

If I said that Iggy kind of told me, she'd completely dismiss me as a quack. "I think he has a bush of it in his backyard."

The lies were compounding. I'd never been to Cliff's house, so I have no idea what he had back there. If he did have Oleander, he'd never eat it.

"Are you saying you believe he ingested the leaves?"

"More like someone injected him with the liquid form of

Oleander." Could Oleander even be liquified? I had no idea, but the commercial blender in the Tiki Hut kitchen could liquify anything.

She shook her head. "I checked his body for needle marks."

"Did you look around the top of his spine?"

The doctor glanced to the side. "I believe so, though if I recall, he had a bit of hair back there. If the needle was thin enough, it's possible I missed it."

I would have suggested she return to the morgue and look again, but I wasn't sure I wanted her to find the real cause of death. "If you want to check, you know where he is."

"Thank you, Glinda, for your concern."

My pulse was racing, and I was beginning to sweat. I needed some fresh air. "I appreciate you taking the time to answer my question."

"Any time."

I quickly left, and then sat in my car for a few minutes—with the air conditioning running—while I figured out my next move. I was sure I was right, but without the medical examiner changing her report, no one would believe me. I was merely a witch and not some trained doctor.

I needed advice on what to do next, so I drove back home and parked. By now, Drake should have returned to his store. It was possible he thought his assistant Trace would be there, only he hadn't been. Because I'd parked in front, I entered through the main entrance.

"Glinda! I was just about to call you. Did you hear the great news about Cliff dying from natural causes?" Drake asked.

"I did. It's wonderful. I bet Jaxson is relieved." I didn't want to burst his bubble of happiness just yet.

My friend sobered. "He is, but he's sort of on a mental rampage right now."

I could figure out why. "You mean this gives him the proof he needs to stay away from Witch's Cove forever."

"Exactly." Drake stilled. "What's wrong? You're not your usually bubbly self. I thought you'd be excited."

"I'm really happy for Jaxson, but I have a dilemma."

He set down the box of crackers and the package of cheese he was about to put in a basket. "I'm listening."

I told him how I just had to find out how Cliff died. "Even my mother saw the crystal change to purple."

Drake said nothing for a moment, but then his jaw tensed, and his eyes shifted right and then left. I could tell he understood my dilemma, especially since he believed in my abilities. "The medical examiner didn't believe you, I take it?"

"No, but given time, she might decide to look at the body again."

He slammed his hand on the counter. "Glinda, can't you see this will give the sheriff a reason to arrest my brother again?"

I sucked in a breath. "Yes, but I am a witch. It's what I do. I couldn't lie—or rather I couldn't hide the truth."

"Not even for me?"

I really wanted to say that I would, but I knew I couldn't. "Not even for my own mother, but you need to find out what proof the sheriff has or doesn't have."

"He has none. I'm sure of it, because my brother didn't kill anyone."

"Then all will be well."

He shoved the crackers and cheese in the basket. "Do what you need to do, but don't expect me to help you." As if a cold front had descended in a matter of minutes, Drake shut me out. I could feel the imaginary knife he'd thrust at me twist in my gut.

"Don't you want to find out who really killed Cliff?" I asked. Of all people, Drake believed in justice.

He faced me. "Normally I do, but in this case? No, and I'm not sure why you do either. You didn't even like Cliff."

"I know, but it's the right thing to do."

Drake shook his head. "Even if the right thing drags my brother down?"

I could see his point, but I had my convictions. "Yes, even if it drags your brother down. We can only hope the courts won't convict him without proof—of which there will be none."

"Fat chance of that."

Not one to do well with conflict, especially with someone I really cared about, I spun around and left. My stomach was about to revolt, and I swear my heart was ripping in two. Before I lost my nerve, I wanted to at least apprise the sheriff of my findings. He'd laugh at me, but that was okay—unless, of course, he knew in his heart that his son had been killed.

I crossed the street and marched right up to the sheriff's department. My hand shook as I pulled open the door.

Pearl looked up and flashed me a brief smile. "This is a nice surprise. Did you get to talk with Buffy?"

To be honest, I'd almost forgotten about her. "Yes, thanks for the lead."

"I'm sorry you wasted your time since we've now learned no one harmed Cliff."

"That's okay." Even though I believed someone had.

I looked behind her for the sheriff, but I didn't see him. Someone in a deputy's uniform was sitting at Cliff's desk though, and for a moment I thought he'd returned from the dead. I shuddered to think I would be seeing Cliff's ghost for the rest of my life. It didn't matter that I didn't even believe in ghosts.

That sealed it. I needed a relaxing beach day.

If the man wasn't a ghost, who was he? Cliff's replacement, perhaps? The deputy wasn't even in the ground yet. Or had the mayor requested him to investigate Cliff's death? If he was here for that, the man had wasted a trip. "Who is that?" I whispered to Pearl.

She grinned. "That's my grandson, Steve Rocker." She twisted around. "Oh, Stevie! Come here. I want you to meet someone." She turned back to me. "He's single, you know."

Oh, no. I didn't have time to date, especially since I was trying to help Drake and Jaxson in my spare time. And no, I would not entertain the idea that Steve Rocker killed Cliff just so he could have the job. That was Penny's imagination working overtime.

The deputy stood. Whoa. I swear he topped six-foot-five and appeared to be quite powerful. And yes, Penny was right about another thing: He was a looker.

He strode over, gave me a pleasant smile, and then held out his hand. "I'm Deputy Rocker."

"Glinda Goodall."

His smile vanished. "How can I help you? Or are you here to chat with my grandmother?"

"No, I came to tell the sheriff something, but since he's not here, you'll do. Can we go somewhere a bit more private in case someone comes in?" In truth, I didn't want Pearl to hear. She'd tell the whole town. If there was a killer on the loose, I didn't need to put a target on my back.

"Sure, follow me." He turned around and then strode toward the back wall, one that was lined with a few offices as well as a conference room. I couldn't help but notice his nice rear. That didn't mean I was interested in him, mind you, but I wasn't blind either.

Steve, or rather Deputy Rocker, led me to a glassed enclosed conference room where he pulled out a chair for me. He walked around the table and sat across from me.

Only then did I notice his intense green eyes, which I had to say, were a bit intimidating.

I cleared my throat, unsure of how to begin. "Are you from around here?" I asked, even though I knew the answer.

His eyebrows rose. "No, though I have visited my grandmother on and off for years, which means I'm not a stranger to Witch's Cove."

"Ah, yes. I remember now. She said you applied for the deputy's job once before."

His forehead creased. "Are you here on behalf of the Witch's Cove gentry to make sure I'm legit, because if you are, I can assure you I am."

On behalf of the gentry? That was funny. We weren't that snobbish. My family might have been in Witch's Cove since the beginning of time, but we never considered ourselves elitists. "No. Just making conversation."

His lips thinned. "I see. You said you needed to discuss something with the sheriff?"

"Yes, it's about Cliff's death."

His shoulders relaxed. "It is very sad that a man that young drops dead, but it happens. Our job is stressful."

"Here's the thing. I believe he was murdered."

I held my breath waiting for the laughter or beratement that was sure to come, but the deputy had no change in emotion. "He was murdered, you say? Interesting. I can show you the medical examiner's report that says otherwise."

"Yes, yes, I know. I just came from speaking with Dr. Sanchez."

His eyes slightly widened, but that was the only sign that he'd heard me. "Did she agree with you?" he asked.

He knew she hadn't, or Dr. Sanchez would have sent over another report. "No."

"I see." From his tone, he thought I was a crackpot. "Were you and Cliff close?" he asked.

I understood why he'd think that. Who else would insist someone had done him in but a girlfriend? Clearly, I was messing this up. "No. It's not like that. Here's the thing. I'm a witch."

Now he chuckled—emotional barrier dropped. "A witch?" He lifted his chin and leaned closer, his eyes searching my face. "I don't see a wart on the end of your nose."

If I had a dime…I didn't take the bait. "Pearl never mentioned we have witches here in Witch's Cove?" The name itself should have given him a hint.

"Yes, but…"

He was a non-believer. I got it. "Whether you believe me or not, it's my obligation to tell you what I found." I relayed my process for determining the cause of death. If he thought I was a kook, at least I'd tried.

"Interesting. Is this the first time you've done this…detection process?"

Once more I was tempted to leave, but that would be impolite. "No. You can speak with Dr. Sanchez. While she was skeptical about my results this time, she has seen my witchcraft work."

He placed his palms on the table. Steve Rocker had really nice hands. "I'll tell you what. I will pass this information along to the sheriff, and he can decide what course of action to take." He pushed back his chair and leaned slightly forward. I so wanted to wipe the smirk off his face.

"Thank you," I said in a professional tone.

I stood, pulled open the door, and walked toward the exit.

"I like your outfit," he called, a sudden rush of cheer in his voice.

Seriously? I did not look back or answer him. "Have a good day, Pearl," I said.

"You too, hon."

After crossing the street, I went in the side entrance of

the Tiki Hut Grill, scurrying along the back wall of the gift shop to reach my stairwell. I was halfway to my apartment when footsteps sounded behind me.

"Glinda, can you come down here? I need to talk to you," my aunt said.

I really wanted to relax, but I could never say no to Aunt Fern. I did an about face. "Sure."

She waited for me in the hallway while I retraced my steps. She placed a hand on my arm, a sure sign she needed a favor. While I would agree to cover for one of the servers who was on the night shift, I really wanted one day without interruption. "What can I do for you?"

"I was hoping you'd already done it. You did remember that you had volunteered to decorate the restaurant for Memorial Day next week, right? We need to remember our fallen soldiers."

Memorial Day. Oh, no. "I kind of forgot."

"Glinda Goodall. You can't have forgotten. I need you."

My mind spun. "Okay, I'll get right on it."

Aunt Fern was always changing up the theme of the Tiki Hut to reflect the season. No sooner would we celebrate Memorial Day then I'd have to decorate for the Fourth of July. Fortunately, we had some decorations from the previous years, but repeating them exactly was forbidden—Aunt Fern's rule.

She smiled. "Thank you, dear. I knew I could count on you."

"I'll look in the storeroom tonight. I promise."

"I appreciate it. I'll sew anything you need. Just let me know."

"Great." That was good since I didn't own a sewing machine. Before I was tasked with something else, I rushed upstairs for some respite. I stepped inside and spotted Iggy sniffing the Oleander branch and the flowers. Are you kidding me? "Iggy. Get away from that."

He spun around. "Just trying to see if I can get any vibes off it."

What did that mean? "Are you sensing something?"

Even after fourteen years, I wasn't sure of his abilities. He was magical, that much I knew.

"Not from this particular branch, but I keep being drawn to it. What did you find out?"

"My necklace told me Cliff was poisoned, but neither the medical examiner nor the new deputy at the sheriff's department believed me. It's just as well, because now Jaxson will not spend another day in jail."

"Back up," Iggy said. "Deputy?"

"Pearl's grandson."

"Ah, Stevie."

This was ridiculous. "How did you hear about him? He just moved here." And his name was Steve, not Stevie. He was no boy.

Iggy tapped his forehead. Okay, he was probably just scratching his face, but it looked like he was trying to indicate how smart he was.

"What's he like?" Iggy asked.

"He's a non-believer and a bigot." I really didn't need any matchmaking from a lizard. I set my purse on the coffee table and then dropped onto the sofa. "I need a one-minute break to think, before I head out again. Aunt Fern asked me to plan the decorations for Memorial Day, and I totally forgot about it. I need to check what we have on hand and then go shopping." Only then could I take a soak in the tub.

"You take that rest, but our discussion about this new deputy is not over."

At this moment, I was tempted to find a spell to send him

back to the forest and let someone else have him. "You won't let it go, will you?"

"Nope. I learned that trait from you."

He'd be right about that.

CHAPTER 9

After dinner, I took the time to search through our storage closet to see what decorations we had on hand. I learned that we desperately needed fabric for tablecloths. The only ones we had were either black or white. The black was too depressing, and the white tablecloths seemed too formal. It was time to go shopping.

Ten minutes later, I pulled into the parking lot of the strip mall where the fabric store was located. As soon as I slipped out of the front seat, who should be coming down the outside staircase but Buffy Bigalow, her son, Dusty, and a tall, wiry, redheaded man. While I ought to just head into the fabric store and mind my own business, I couldn't. I mean, that wouldn't have been neighborly of me, right?

I made a beeline over to Buffy. "Hey, your cheek is looking better," I said, trying to sound positive.

She averted her gaze. "Thanks."

From her unenthusiastic response, that might not have been the best topic to bring up, especially since a former boyfriend had hit her. I held out my hand to the stranger.

"I'm Glinda Goodall. I work at the Tiki Hut Grill. You should stop in some time."

"Greg Anderson." From his terse sounding comment, he had no desire to socialize.

Ah, the boyfriend from Morganville. Normally, I might have smiled, turned, and rushed into the fabric store, but I wanted to prolong this meeting in order to get a sense of him. "You staying long, Greg?"

"No."

Clearly, the man wasn't receptive to my questions. Fine. I could take a hint. I turned to Buffy. "I best be going," I said.

When she didn't say anything, I spun around and headed to the fabric store. After spending a minute in there, I peeked out again to see what the three of them were doing, but they were gone. It was probably for the best. I had a job to do. Being surrounded by the pretty colors, lush fabrics, and rows of buttons and threads, it sucked the tension right out of my body. I'd forgotten how much I loved fabric shopping.

It didn't take me long to find some thick cotton material. I picked up a bit of red and some blue fabric and then decided I could reuse a few of the white cloths that we already had. Once I cut the material to size for the tablecloths, I'd ask Aunt Fern to hem the edges.

When I spotted camouflage material, I decided it would look great as a skirt for around the coffee station table. We had a ton of small flags in the storage room that I planned to place in the flower vases that were already on each table. After I figured out how much material I needed, I waited for the woman to cut the yardage.

"What are you making?" she asked.

"Mostly tablecloths. The Tiki Hut Grill wants to honor those fallen on Memorial Day."

"How nice."

She took forever, being careful to give me the exact

amount I requested. Once I had the fabric, I grabbed some matching thread, a ton of red, white, and blue seam binding and paid for my purchases. With my bags of fabric in hand, I headed out.

Now that I'd finished my investigation of Cliff Duncan, there was nothing more I could do—or needed to do. He'd died of natural causes, so it made no sense to ask any more questions. For now, I'd enjoy drawing up a plan to decorate the Grill and hope that Drake eventually forgave me.

Once back at my apartment, I dumped all of my packages on the sofa.

"What's all that?" Iggy asked.

"It's the fabric for the tablecloths. I thought I told you Aunt Fern asked me to do the decorations for Memorial Day." Iggy normally never forgot anything. I explained my idea on how I wanted to decorate.

"You should hire a singer to play military songs. That could be a nice draw. And you should also have some women in skimpy outfits. I bet the service men, past and present, would like that."

"That's actually not a bad idea—the singer part, not the women dressed in skimpy outfits part. Remember we are a family restaurant, and Memorial Day is a day of reflection about honoring the fallen men. Because Aunt Fern gives free meals to any veteran or active duty member, we'll be packed all day." She did the same thing for Veterans Day.

"Cool. She should do that for Iguana Day."

I laughed. "Don't count on it. Besides, there is no such thing as Iguana Day."

"Then there should be. I'm going to lobby Aunt Fern for one."

"You do that."

Because I was beat, I took a shower, crawled into bed, and grabbed my e-reader. I wanted to forget most of what happened today. Tomorrow, I would cut the fabric for the tables and recruit a few fellow workers to help me decide where to put the other decorations.

As soon as I clocked in the next morning, Penny rushed up to me. "I need a favor."

"What is it?"

She inhaled deeply. "It's Sam. Something is going on with him."

"What happened?" I grabbed a half empty sugar container and filled it.

"He got in a fight last night, and I don't want him to pick up Tommy from school looking the way he does. He has a shiner and a split lip, and that won't set a good example for our son."

"I agree." I could guess what her request would be. "You should pick him up from school. I'll cover for you." She didn't need to leave until two, so I'd only be covering for the last hour.

Penny hugged me. "You are the best."

"Did Sam tell you who he fought?" I did like gossip.

"He was rather vague. He mumbled something about him having a partner when he lived elsewhere. Somehow, things went wrong between them, and then Sam moved here."

"I take it money was involved?" I asked.

"That would be my guess, but he won't talk about it. He's too embarrassed, I think."

"Could it have been drugs?" I asked.

"Shh. Probably. He got into steroids pretty heavily after we were married. He fancied himself a bodybuilder and spent more time in the gym than he did at home, though I never saw much improvement. It was one of the reasons I left him. I didn't want Tommy exposed to anything like that."

"Smart." It was always possible Sam never made it to the gym, but who am I to say? Working out was never my thing.

"Ladies?" my aunt called. "Are we working today or chatting?"

"Working," I shot back.

I returned to filling the sugar containers as well as topping off the condiments while Penny made the coffee.

The morning crowd was steady, but it tapered off around ten thirty, and it didn't pick up again until noon. I was busy running between the tables and the kitchen when Aunt Fern called me to the cashier's counter.

"Why don't you take table two?" my aunt asked with a grin on her face.

I spun around and almost sighed out loud when I saw it was the new deputy. "I'll ask Penny to take it."

"She's busy."

I was too stressed to argue with her. "Sure."

The deputy was watching us, and I could only guess what he was thinking. In all honesty, I'm surprised he wanted to talk to me again. He didn't believe in witches and seemed to think I was a kook.

"Deputy, what can I get you?" I asked with my pen poised.

"What's good here?"

"Let me see. The crab cakes are spectacular, and the hamburgers are pure sirloin, but we are known for our Shephard's Pie."

"I'll take the Shephard's Pie then and a coffee, black."

"You got it." I turned around as quickly as I could.

"Glinda?"

I stilled, inhaled in order to paint on a smile, and faced him again. "Yes?"

"I wonder if you could do me a favor?"

My mind raced trying to think if I'd missed some *Do a favor for a friend national holiday* or something—except he wasn't my friend. "What is it?"

"The father of a friend of mine died yesterday in my hometown."

"I'm sorry."

He leaned on his elbows. "Here's the thing. The man's doctor is saying that because he had a heart condition, he died of a heart attack."

I didn't know where he was going with this. "But you think otherwise?"

"Yes. As does my friend. He even requested an autopsy." He explained that the father repaired roofs for a living.

"You're telling me this, why?" I asked.

He pressed his lips together and then sat up straighter. "I want you to try your magic on him before the medical examiner opens him up."

If I'd been drinking anything, it would have been all over him. "You want the crackpot witch to determine how he died? Why? A medical examiner will do a much more accurate job than I ever could." That wasn't necessarily the case, but because I'd never convince him of that, why try?

"That may be, but I want to be sure she doesn't miss something. Your analysis might give her a starting point."

Boy, Deputy Rocker must be desperate if he was asking me. I have to admit it took guts on his part. Even if I didn't say anything to anyone, the word would get out. It always did in this town. I was about to turn him down, but then thought better of it. It would be sweet if I had an ally in the sheriff's department. Not getting a lot of blowback for my theories would be a refreshing change. "Sure. When do you want to do this? I get off work at three."

"How about I pick you up at three thirty then? It's about a two-hour drive."

Second thoughts flooded me. I wasn't sure I could ride in a car with him for a total of four hours. It would unnerve me, but I certainly wouldn't admit that. I needed to be cool. "No problem. I'll be ready. Let me put in your order."

I rushed toward the kitchen, angry at myself for letting him sway me. It must have been those green eyes of his. Or was I still stinging from everyone's rejection over my most recent analysis that I was willing to do anything to prove myself? Could I really be that shallow?

No. I agreed, because I needed Steve Rocker on my side. Besides, if I had to spend a few hours with him, I could learn more about him—like whether Rocker was his real name. Maybe it was short for Rockefeller. He could be some rich recluse.

I shook my head at how ridiculous I sounded, even to myself. Not wanting to look like a complete fool, I wouldn't ask him—at least on this trip.

One of my many flaws was my ability to obsess over things, and I needed to stop. I dropped off his order and then checked on my other tables. When I returned to the kitchen, Penny rushed up to me. "Why did you take table two? I would have waited on the cute deputy."

I should have said that Aunt Fern was playing matchmaker, but I didn't want there to be any stress between those two. "He asked for me. He wants me to do an analysis on the father of a friend who died."

"He's probably using that as an excuse. I bet he just wants to date you," Penny said.

That made me laugh. "I don't think so. There is no chemistry between us. Personally, I think he is testing me."

Penny smiled. "Testing to see if you'll go out with him."

I didn't need to be discussing this. "I need to check on his food."

Happy to get away from another matchmaker, I picked up

the deputy's order and delivered it. "Enjoy," I said as I placed his bill on the table. "Take your time."

He smiled. "Thank you."

Once more that smile and those eyes did something to me, and I wasn't happy about it. While I didn't do spells very often, I needed to put one on myself to block his allure. I turned around and was thankful when one of my tables had new customers to keep me occupied for a while.

The deputy ate quickly and left without asking for anything else. To my surprise, he gave me a nice tip. I debated giving the extra money back to him when we went to his hometown—wherever that was—but he might take it the wrong way. This was a professional trip and nothing more.

By three, I was pretty frazzled, since I had my tables as well as Penny's for the last hour. Because it was rather sticky and humid outside, most of the new arrivals opted to eat indoors. Ray Zink, who usually only worked the patio, offered to help inside.

"You are a lifesaver," I told him.

"I'm happy to get out of the heat."

"No matter your reason, I appreciate it." Before I clocked out, I told him I was meeting someone at three thirty and had to shower and change. "Could you refill the sugar, salt, and pepper shakers, as well as the condiment bottles so I could leave a minute or two early?"

"Happy to oblige."

"I owe you one," I said.

"No problem."

Ray was forty, married with two kids, and an army vet with PTSD. Even though he was trained as a computer expert, he took this job because he said it was low stress. I didn't agree with him, but I was glad he worked at the Tiki Hut.

Needing to change out of my costume, I rushed upstairs. As soon as I stepped inside, Iggy perked up. "You're a bit stressed, I see."

I didn't have time to fully explain what I was going to do tonight, so I gave him the shortened version. "I've been asked to do another analysis on a body. Because it's in another town, I won't be back until it's late. Excuse me. I have to shower and change."

I rushed to my bedroom, tossed my pink crown on the bed, ditched my shoes, and stripped. After a quick shower, I pulled on some light pink jeans and a loose-fitting dark rose long-sleeve shirt in case Deputy Rocker decided to crank up the air in his car. I then stepped into my pink high tops. I didn't give my outfit a second look, and I refused to put on makeup. This wasn't a date.

Three minutes to go. Iggy was blocking my way into the hallway. "I don't want to be late."

"You usually do your magic at your parents' funeral home."

"True, but this is a special case. The deputy asked that I go with him to his hometown. Rocker claims he wants to make sure the medical examiner does a thorough job, but I think he just wants to see if I have any talent. He might be waffling over Cliff's death being from natural causes."

Iggy shook his head. "You are so in denial."

"About what?" I didn't have time for this. Keeping someone waiting was rude.

"It's a date."

"A date, huh? It's not. Now please move."

From his erect posture, he was offended. It was my fault that I'd raised him to be overly curious like myself.

"Have fun," he finally said.

"Being in the room with a dead body is never fun."

CHAPTER 10

"I wasn't sure you were going to show." The deputy was waiting for me by the front entrance of the Grill.

"Why would you think that?"

"You're five minutes late."

He had to be kidding. "I just got off work, and I really needed to shower and change." Sheesh. Control freak much?

The deputy held up a hand. "I'm sorry. I was being insensitive. I know this is your time to relax, and instead, you are going to spend a few hours with me to examine a dead body."

At least he understood that I was doing him a favor. "Dead bodies I'm used to. Driving half way across Florida with a stranger, I am not."

He tossed me a brief smile. "I'm not dangerous. I am the law."

How many times had someone fallen victim to that line of thinking?

"I know." I only said that because this conversation was making me uncomfortable.

He held open the restaurant's front door and led me to a

black Range Rover that I assumed was his personal car. I had been worried we'd be taking Cliff's cruiser. That would have been too weird.

I was glad the new deputy didn't open the car door for me. That meant this was business and nothing more—unless his mother hadn't raised him right.

The first few minutes of the trip were fine since he didn't try to make idle conversation. Every time I looked over at him, his eyes were on the road, which was something I appreciated. But riding in silence for two hours wasn't my style either. My mouth wasn't capable of staying shut for that long, so I went on the offensive.

"Where is your hometown?" I wanted to text Penny my destination in case I never came back.

"Overton. It's about two hours northeast of Witch's Cove."

He'd mentioned before that it would take that long. "Did you grow up there?"

He glanced over at me. "Is this going to be another inquisition?" At least he was kind of smiling when he asked me.

"No, just making conversation."

He nodded. "Fair enough. Here's my life story summed up in a thirty second sound bite. I was born in Overton. When I was fifteen, my mom passed away. After high school, I enlisted in the Marines and served for four years. When I came home, I proposed to my high school sweetheart."

Stop the presses! I had totally misread this guy. "You're married?"

"Not anymore. I'm getting to that. After my four years in the service, I went to school at the University of Florida for a degree in criminology. Even though I drove home on weekends and every holiday, it didn't work out between us." Steve —if I could be so bold to call him that—shifted in his seat. He wasn't telling me everything, but now wasn't the time to call him on it.

"I'm sorry."

"Yeah, me too. It happens. Anyway, I felt the need for some space so I came to Witch's Cove to see if they might be interested in having another deputy."

"Did your grandmother imply there might be an opening?"

Steve tossed her a quick smile. "Yes, but clearly she overstated the need for more law enforcement here."

"Pearl was probably lonely and wanted you here."

Steve looked over at her again. "You seem to know her well."

Was that a compliment? If it was, I'd take it. Getting in good with him was one of my goals for this trip. "Witch's Cove is a small town. Everyone knows just about everything about its residents."

"I'll keep that in mind."

As always, I wasn't able to stop digging. "I heard Cliff wasn't very welcoming to you when you showed up." Even though I no longer suspected Steve of harming Cliff in order to get the job, I did want to hear his side of the story.

"No, he wasn't. Our interaction was, shall we say, strained. I think he liked being the only deputy."

I could see that. "After you didn't get the job, what did you do?"

"I debated not going back to Overton, but my dad wasn't in the best of health, so I returned home and found a job as a security guard. Because I planned to leave once he felt better, I didn't apply for a job at the sheriff's department." His grip tightened on the wheel. "I have to say I was never so bored in my life. Standing around is not my style."

"I would hate that too. I enjoy interacting with people."

"I can see that. Now that you know about me, what's your story, Glinda Goodall?"

I'd already told him I was a witch, so there wasn't much to add. "My life is pretty dull compared to yours. After high school, I went to the University of Central Florida where I earned my degree in math with a concentration in statistics."

"For real?" I wouldn't say his tone was insulting, but it implied that a waitress couldn't be educated.

"Yes. As for why I am working in my aunt's restaurant, let's just say jobs aren't plentiful for someone with my skills. I wasn't into accounting, so that line of work was out. I did accept a middle school teaching position out of town, but after giving it a year, I decided it wasn't my thing."

"I bet you'd be a great teacher."

That was the last thing I expected him to say. "I'm sure my students would disagree."

"Kids can be cruel." There was a lot of pain in his voice, but I wasn't ready to delve into his issues. I had enough of my own.

"They were mostly only cruel to each other. I think only one of the kids actually liked math. The rest thought it was useless."

I expected him to ask when the last time was that I used math, but he didn't, and I have to say I was relieved. Once we exhausted my life's story, we chatted a bit about the various people in Witch's Cove—who the movers and shakers were, and who he should keep an eye on.

Close to five thirty we arrived in Overton. It was a quaint town, not much bigger than Witch's Cove. Instead of having a beach though, it was surrounded by miles of forest. I liked it. On the far edge of town was the hospital, and Steve parked in the lot.

"I forgot to ask. How can you just prance in and ask to see a body?"

"I have friends in high places." He winked.

That worked for me. I piled out of the cruiser and followed him inside. I guess his uniform was good enough to get us to the morgue. He knocked on a secured door, and a few seconds later a pretty woman answered. "Steve! You made it." The woman, who was probably in her fifties, held out her hand to me. "I'm Doctor Arnold."

"I'm Glinda Goodall. Nice to meet you."

With the pleasantries out of the way, she escorted us inside. "Would it be okay for me to watch you do your magic?" she asked. "I've never even heard of anything like this."

"Sure." What could I say? This was her morgue, though if I'd gone to med school, I doubt I'd be interested in learning what an untrained person had to say. It was nice that she was willing to give it a try. Few people of science were.

"Would you like the body on the table here?" she asked.

"Yes, please." I removed my necklace and squeezed it tight, hoping my nerves wouldn't interfere with my magic. After taking a few deep breaths, my pulse slowed. I was ready. Because I had an audience, I thought it best to talk through my procedure.

The corpse before me appeared to be in his late fifties to early sixties. Without any medical skills, I needed to ignore anything else about him, like his rather weathered face and rough hands and feet. Inhaling once more, I dangled the pendant over his feet. "I like to start at the bottom and work my way up," I announced.

I performed the same method that I had for Cliff, readjusting the sheet to give me access to his skin. Nothing happened until I reached his ribcage. Steve had said the cause of death was probably a heart attack, but instead of seeing the expected green color to indicate a blockage, the stone shone red. I looked up at the doctor. "I'm detecting some internal bleeding and possible bruising."

"I only briefly looked at the body. At the time, I didn't see any skin discoloration," the doctor said.

When the stone returned to pink rather quickly, I figured the bleeding wasn't what had killed him. "Interesting," I said.

"What?" Steve asked.

"His heart isn't giving me any hint of green, which leads me to think he didn't die of a heart attack." When I swung the stone over his forehead, it flashed red, which gave me an idea. "Can you roll him over?" I asked.

I stepped back and let the medical examiner and Steve move him. I then swung the stone over the back of the man's head, and sure enough it turned very dark red. "Well, I'll be."

"What did that mean?" the doctor asked.

"Does red mean more bleeding or bruising?" Steve asked.

I was impressed he'd caught on so quickly. "Yes. A brain bleed, perhaps." As much as I wanted to move his matted hair to see if there was any blood, I didn't dare touch the body. "Is it possible this man received a blow to the back of the head?" I asked.

"I will definitely check that when I do the autopsy."

"I mentioned that Ralph here works construction," Steve said.

"Roofing."

"Yes. He has to be on the hot roof for long periods. I suppose he could have fallen off, though my friend Jake never said anything about that." He glanced at the doctor.

"I rule nothing out, but I would have expected more bruising and maybe even a broken bone or two if he took a tumble," Dr. Arnold said.

Steve's shoulders sagged a bit, though I'm not sure why.

I've never believed I was clairvoyant or anything, but a scenario flashed in my mind. "If it was hot on the roof, is it possible this man was feeling faint, came down, and then passed out. He could have fallen against a bench and bruised his ribs. After resting, he went home and thought he was okay, but the damage had already been done. Is it possible that was why you didn't notice any bruising?" I asked the medical examiner.

The doctor's mouth opened and then shut. "It certainly is possible. I've heard of men having brain bleeds and thinking their symptoms were due to dehydration."

"Would you like me to repeat my procedure?" I asked.

"You don't need to bother. I appreciate you coming all this way."

"Thank you for letting me take a look first. I hope you find the cause of death," I said. That was a dumb thing to say, but it had made me a little nervous to have a professional watch me.

"I hope so too. This was fascinating to watch you work. When I perform the autopsy tomorrow, I will take care to check out his ribs and head for any signs of a bleed. I'll write up my report and send Jake a copy."

"I'll ask him for a copy," Steve said. "Thanks." As soon as we exited, Steve turned to me. "That was amazing."

Heat raced up my face. The only people who had ever watched me do my magic were my mom and Penny, and both assumed I knew what I was doing. "Don't get your hopes up too much. My system isn't foolproof."

"Good to know." We made our way out of the hospital and into the warm, fresh air. "Jake will be happy to know his dad might not have died of a heart attack," Steve said.

He did believe me! "I'd wait for the autopsy report, but I tend to believe my stone. You said Jake thought his dad was injured on the job?"

"Yes. Ralph told him the night he passed away that he probably should retire since the heat was getting to him. He was sick for two days before he died. Sure, he had a bad heart, but he was on medication for it."

"I hope Dr. Arnold learns the truth."

"Me too, but if the company Ralph worked for failed to warn him of the dangers, Jake will want to go after them. Too bad that won't bring his dad back."

"If the dad had a heart condition, wouldn't his doctor have told him of the risks of climbing on hot roofs?"

"Probably. I don't think Jake is being upfront with me about all of the facts—or else his dad didn't come clean with his son."

Steve really seemed to want to help his friend. "If only we had witch's in our town who could revive the dead, so much sorrow could be avoided."

"That would be amazing if they could." Steve glanced at his watch. "It's six now. Want to grab something to eat before we drive back?"

I was starving, though that was no surprise. I was usually hungry. Being surrounded by food all day did that to me. "Sure."

Steve drove out of town, possibly because he didn't want to be spotted by anyone. Either his dad or his ex-wife might wonder why he hadn't stopped by or called if they learned he'd returned. I could relate. Sometimes I wanted to avoid a lot of questions too.

When we drove to a fast food place rather than to a nice sit-down restaurant, it reinforced that this hadn't been a date in any sense of the word. It also meant I'd be home at a reasonable hour.

"Let's go inside. I don't like to eat and drive."

"Works for me."

Inside, I ordered a chicken Caesar salad and a sweet tea.

"That's all?" Steve asked. "I'm buying."

I had to laugh. "If I ate what I wanted all the time, I'd need a seatbelt extension."

"You would not."

"You'd be surprised," I said. "I just smell food and the pounds pour on. I have to be careful."

Steve was smart enough to keep his opinion to himself. He ordered two hamburgers, a large order of fries, a chocolate shake, and three chocolate chip cookies. Seriously? The man didn't have an ounce of fat on him—not that I had noticed.

Throughout the meal, I said nothing, until I couldn't hold back any longer. "By any chance did you mention my thoughts on Cliff's death to the sheriff?"

"I did."

"And?"

"He said he would look into it."

Even with my suggestion of poison, the sheriff wouldn't have any idea where to look though. "I think Cliff might have been poisoned with Oleander."

"Oleander? Did your stone turn some color to indicate that?"

"No, but I have a feeling about it."

Steve dipped his chin. "A feeling? As in you experienced some psychic connection with Cliff?"

I could see I was losing him, but I couldn't tell him about Iggy. I wasn't so naïve to think that if Steve Rocker didn't believe in witchcraft that he wouldn't recognize familiars were real either. Even if he met Iggy, once he realized he couldn't communicate with him, he'd never believe I could talk to my iguana. "Not me, but my mother can talk to the dead."

"Your mother?"

"Yes." I'd pretty much had enough of his skepticism. "You

know, if you want to fit in to your new town, you need to be a bit more open-minded about the occult."

"I'm plenty open-minded. I asked you to look at Ralph's body, didn't I?"

"Yes, you did. Well then, if you are so *open-minded*, you should ask a psychic to help you solve crimes."

His eyebrows rose. "You don't say. Did you ask a psychic about Cliff's death?"

"Not yet. Once the medical examiner said it wasn't murder, I let it go."

"I'm no psychic, but I don't believe you're the type to let anything go."

Darn. He was a bit too perceptive. "I should have said I'm trying to let it go."

Steve grinned. "That's what I thought."

After we finished eating, we tossed the bags in the trash, and returned to his car.

He didn't say much until we'd driven a good fifteen minutes. "You said your mother can connect psychically with the dead?"

"Yes."

"Did she try to speak with Cliff?"

"She did."

"What did Cliff say?" he asked.

I didn't want to arm him with anything else that he could criticize, but he had asked, so I told him what my mother had said.

He looked over at me and smiled. "Did Cliff happen to say that he was now in a happy place?"

"Are you talking about heaven?" I asked.

"I guess I am."

"I couldn't say. Perhaps you should speak with my mom about its existence." I don't know why I was being a jerk, but when someone put down anyone in our town, I had the need to defend them.

"I just might."

"I'm hoping I can convince the sheriff to ask Dr. Sanchez to recheck her findings," I said, curious how Steve would respond.

"That would be great if she did."

If that happened, I would have to say I'd accomplished my mission. Score one for the home team.

CHAPTER 11

After Steve dropped me off at the restaurant, my mind wouldn't stop spinning; doubt was chasing me. What if my analysis of his friend's dad was wrong? I was just glad there would be an autopsy to prove or disprove my theory. Regardless of whether I was right or wrong, during this trip I believed I'd opened the deputy's eyes to the reality that witches not only existed, but that some of us had real powers.

Admittedly, when I'd suggested he contact a psychic, he wasn't exactly receptive. I had to remember to take baby steps. I should have at least given him Gertrude Poole's name in case he changed his mind. She might be close to ninety, but she was one wise woman.

Why I hadn't sought her help before, I wasn't sure. Maybe I should now—at least with regard to what happened to Cliff.

"How was your trip to Overton?" Aunt Fern asked as I reached the landing to my apartment. Probably having heard my heavy feet on the creaking steps, she'd opened her door and stepped into the rather dim hallway where our doors faced each other.

"How did you hear about that?"

She tilted her head to the side. "Why Iggy, of course. He couldn't wait to tell me the latest gossip."

I needed to buy a muzzle for him. Only kidding, but he was old enough to know when he should keep his mouth shut. "How did you know I was going to Overton? Even I didn't know before I left."

"Tsk, tsk. Ye of little faith. There are a host of people in town who have the 411 on the cute sheriff."

411? Aunt Fern knew that expression? "Did Pearl tell you?"

"I'll admit I called her. Now tell me everything."

I wouldn't have any peace until I gave her a brief rundown, so I gave her a few details. "I'm not sure the deputy is any closer to believing in witches than he was before I went with him." Okay, maybe a little closer. At least he hadn't mocked my results this time.

She grinned. "He'll come around."

I blew out a breath. "Aunt Fern, I don't want him to come around. I just want a bit of respect."

"Oh, I'm sure he respects you all right. Good night." She wiggled her fingers and then grinned before ducking back into her apartment.

I was convinced there was a hidden meaning in her comment, but I was too tired to think about it. When I opened my door, Iggy was doing circles on the floor. "What's going on?" I asked.

"It's about time you got back."

"Excuse me?"

"You spent five minutes telling Aunt Fern everything. You had to know I'd be dying to hear how it went."

I chuckled. "You didn't hear the conversation through the cat door?"

"This time I did, but you should have opened it up and invited me to join you."

I didn't need his attitude right now. He went through the cat door on a daily basis. If he wanted to hear what I had to say, he should have just joined us. "I need to shower. Then I'm crawling into bed."

"See if I help you with a crime again."

Something was up. Even though I probably smelled of death, I grabbed a glass of water and then dropped down on the sofa. "Fine. Tell me what's going on."

Iggy jumped up next to me. "While you were on your date, I was doing real detective work."

"If your ego were any bigger, your eyes would fall out of your head."

Iggy shut his lids. "Tell me that's a lie."

How could such a cute animal be so smart and so naïve at the same time. "Yes, I was kidding." He hit me with his tail, and it stung. "Hey, watch it, Mr. Sleuth."

He stilled. "Mr. Sleuth? I like it. Maybe you can buy me a new collar, one with an engraved gold nameplate instead of this stupid pink collar."

It wasn't stupid. "You look cute in the pink bowtie. Now tell me what you found out."

"Remember you told me about Buffy's ex-boyfriend, the one you ran into at the fabric store?"

"Greg Anderson. What about him?"

"I saw him with Sam around five o'clock. They were arguing in front of the liquor store, and I saw Greg shove Sam."

While I had a view of the street from my bedroom, I doubt the man with Sam was Greg. "You've never met Buffy's ex-boyfriend. You can't know what he looks like."

"No, but how many six-foot-two skinny redheads are in this town?"

"I don't know." I had described Greg to Iggy, so maybe it was him. While Iggy had excellent hearing, he wouldn't have been able to tell what they were arguing about through a closed window. "I'll ask Penny to ask Sam, though I bet he'll deny that he was in another altercation."

"Also have her ask Sam about what he handed the guy."

"What did you see? Money changing hands? Drugs? A phone? What? You need to be specific."

Iggy dropped down to this stomach. "I don't know. Sam's body blocked my view."

I couldn't stand to see Iggy dejected. "It sounds like an excellent lead. I will check it out." I pushed up to a stand. "I'm cleaning up. Did you get enough to eat tonight?"

"Aunt Fern fed me."

Sometimes I wonder if Iggy would even miss me if I were gone. I went into my bedroom and closed the door. I didn't need any more of my familiar tonight.

After I showered, I was not only cleaner, I was more relaxed. However, I wouldn't be able to sleep unless I spoke with Penny and asked her if she knew anything about Sam's discussion with a tall, skinny guy with red hair. Tomorrow, she'd want all of the details about my trip to Overton anyway, so I might as well tell her everything.

"Penny, how is it going?" I asked once she picked up.

"I was just about to call you. How did your date with Mr. Hottie go?"

Why couldn't people leave it alone. "It wasn't a date."

"Whatever. Tell me all about it."

I went into detail about our conversations and then how his friend's dad might have died. "The medical examiner watched me, because she was actually interested in my process and what I discovered. Dr. Arnold said that when she does her autopsy tomorrow, she'll pay particular attention to the brain."

"That's great. How did Deputy Rocker react to your talents?"

That should be talent, not talents. The teasing came through loud and clear. "I think he is one step closer to being a believer."

"Awesome. When are you going out again?"

She wasn't listening. "We aren't." I needed to change the subject. "Hey, Iggy told me something interesting."

"What is it?" Penny finally sounded like her often-worried self.

"He claims he saw Sam and a tall redheaded man get into a small altercation outside of the liquor store this evening. I know you've never met Buffy's ex-boyfriend from Morganville, but is it possible this is the same man who roughed up Sam the other day?"

"Morganville?" The snap of her fingers came through rather loudly. "I must have spaced out when Buffy said the name of the town. Sam lived there for a while before I met him."

That couldn't be a coincidence. "Do you think it's possible that Sam knew Greg Anderson from when he lived there?"

"It's possible."

I needed to pursue this further. "After the yelling fest ended, Iggy thought he saw Sam give Greg something. Could you ask your ex about that too?"

"That might not be the best idea." She hesitated. "We aren't in a real good place right now."

The worry in her voice concerned me. "Penny, what aren't you telling me?"

"Sam has been out of sorts lately."

I tried to decode what that meant. "Are you afraid of him or something?"

"Kind of. I mean, he's great with Tommy, but in the last

few days, he's changed. It's like some kind of evil being has taken over his body."

While I believed my mom could talk to the dead, I wasn't so sure people could actually be possessed by another, and neither did Penny for that matter. It was possible I was being narrow minded like our new deputy. "What happened exactly?"

"I haven't spent all that much time with him, but every time I make even the tiniest of suggestions, he practically jumps down my throat."

"I know you said he wasn't taking any kind of drugs anymore but could something have changed?"

She said nothing for a few seconds. "Maybe seeing Greg again—assuming they knew each other from Morganville—stirred up some memories, especially if there was bad blood between them. Even if Sam were taking drugs again, he wouldn't tell me. It's not like we're married anymore."

My pulse raced. "Did Sam ever mention this redheaded man to you?"

I wished we were talking in person. I would have been able to read her better.

"No, but he admitted that his past was a bit shady."

"Shady how?" I asked.

"He didn't say, but he swore he'd never been arrested. While that might be true, I wouldn't be surprised if he was involved in something bad when he was younger, especially considering the scars on his body."

Ouch. "You mentioned he had a partner of some kind. Could he have been a redheaded one?" It was a stretch, but worth asking.

"I don't know. When we first met, he mentioned someone by the name of Victor, not Greg."

I should have been more relieved, but I wasn't. "How about I ask Steve to check out Greg Anderson?"

"Sure."

"It might be best if you don't mention what Iggy saw to Sam."

"I agree."

This conversation was giving me a stomach ache. "I'll see you tomorrow. And try not to stress, you hear?"

"Like that is going to happen."

I chuckled at that. Not letting go of stress was both of our downfalls.

THE NEXT DAY, I decided I wasn't quite ready to march into the sheriff's office and ask to speak with Steve until I had something a bit more concrete to present to him. I know I said I'd ask about Greg Anderson, but I needed a reason for Steve to investigate.

I had to admit that every time the front door to the Tiki Hut opened though, I thought the deputy would walk in to either tell me about the results of his friend's father's autopsy or to grab a bite to eat.

At one, the sheriff showed up instead. It wasn't surprising that since his son had recently passed away, the sheriff had bags under his eyes, and his uniform looked as if he'd slept in it. For the first time, I actually felt sorry for the guy—for real this time.

Since he sat in my section, I served him. "Sheriff. How are you doing?"

"Not so good, Glinda. Not so good at all."

"Is it because your new deputy mentioned my theory about Cliff's death to you?"

"It's not that. In fact, I never believed my son just dropped dead. I can't disagree with you that he was murdered either.

I've been talking to every person Cliff arrested, and none of them seemed to have held a big enough grudge against my son to kill him."

Did he really expect a killer to admit he wanted Cliff dead? Sheriff Duncan had clearly lost it. While I rarely ever sat with a customer, I needed to make an exception. I pulled out the chair and sat down. "Here's the thing. I'm not sure if this will help at all, but I think Cliff might have been poisoned with Oleander."

"Steve mentioned that too." His voice came out flat.

I totally understood depression, but he was the sheriff. He needed to push back his chair, and start identifying the location of every colorful, poisonous bush in town. On the other hand, he might have decided that would be useless since that plant was everywhere.

"What about Sam Carsted?" I asked. "I have no proof he was involved, but something seems to be going on with him."

As soon as I said his name, my skin heated and guilt swamped me. This was my best girlfriend's ex-husband and the father of her son. I should just keep my mouth shut.

"I know Cliff brought him in a few times. What do you know?"

Penny—the queen of perfect timing—pranced over. "Hi, Sheriff."

"Penny. How are you doing?" he asked.

Dang it. Had she heard me mention her ex-husband's name?" I stood and pulled out my pad. "Sheriff, what can I get you? The usual?"

"Sure." He seemed to understand that I didn't want to talk in front of Penny, and I was glad she had interrupted me before I could say anything else about either of Sam's two quarrels.

I rushed off to drop my ticket at the kitchen window. What had I been thinking mentioning Sam Carsted to the sheriff? Okay, I hadn't been in a good mental place. I realized that my comment might affect Penny, but that redheaded man gave me the creeps.

I sensed Buffy could shed some light on Greg, but most likely the two of them would be together, preventing her from saying anything useful.

For once, I needed to drop my investigation regarding Cliff's death. My original goal had been to clear Jaxson Henderson's name, and now that Cliff's passing had been ruled a death by natural causes, Jaxson was free. I needed to let it be.

Besides, I had a restaurant to decorate. I might even take Iggy's suggestion and hire someone to sing on Memorial Day. But sing what? War songs? How uplifting could that be? Sheesh.

What I really needed to do was take a vacation—far from Witch's Cove—so I wouldn't be tempted to interfere in any investigation. Quitting my teaching job might not have been smart. At least the school year had a two-week vacation at Christmas, a week-long spring break, and two months off over the summer. Since it was May, I could have been looking at a lot of time off in the near future, which sounded very appealing right about now.

While I was ready to finally move on and forget about Cliff Duncan, Penny didn't seem to be. She kept looking at me for the rest of my shift, as if she had overheard me mention Sam's name to the sheriff. Great. My two best friends were mad at me. It didn't matter that I hadn't told the sheriff much. The only positive in my life since Cliff had died was that both of the lawmen in town were actually taking my theory about Cliff's death a bit more seriously.

Truth was, I did almost stab Penny in the back. I had been about to spill the beans about Sam's altercation with the redheaded man to the sheriff because I wanted to shift the sheriff's focus off of Jaxson Harrison and onto Sam Carsted. Since I had no proof of anything, the whole idea was ridiculous and wrong. As far as I knew, Sam wasn't violent, and other than him not liking Cliff, I had no proof that he even wished the deputy dead.

For the next hour, I worked hard to keep busy, and by some miracle, Penny and I managed to avoid each other. When I had a break and went to look for her to explain, she was gone. It wouldn't have surprised me if Penny had to pick up Tommy from school, because either Sam wasn't able to or his bruises hadn't healed from his last fight. Still, she should have told me.

To make sure I wasn't jumping to conclusions about where Penny went, I strode up to Aunt Fern. "Do you know why Penny isn't here?"

"She had to pick up Tommy. Why?"

"She didn't ask me to cover for her."

My aunt nodded toward Ray who was coming in from the outside patio. "She asked him to help out."

Ray? And not her best friend—or rather the person who used to be her best friend? "Great."

I turned back around because I didn't want Aunt Fern to see how hurt I was. I'd totally botched everything, and I needed to fix things—just as soon as I figured out the decorations for Memorial Day, which was in a few days.

I wasn't sure when Cliff's funeral would be held, but between that and Memorial Day, it seemed as if everything was crashing down on me at once. What I really needed was some time off.

CHAPTER 12

The next day was Saturday. I had it off since I'd switched days with Corinne. Instead of enjoying a day at the beach, I had to spend it working on the Memorial Day decorations. It wasn't as if I could put it off any longer. Time was running out. Aunt Fern said she'd sew the hems on the tablecloths tomorrow, but I was responsible for setting up everything else.

Thankfully, she had declared we'd close an hour early on Sunday—at midnight instead of one A.M. so we could set up for the festivities. My aunt had asked a few of the late-night staff to stay and help. It would have been quite difficult to do much when there were people seated at the tables.

Just as I was about to cut the material for the tablecloths, my cell rang. It was my mother. I hoped she hadn't changed her mind about being the one to prepare Cliff's body for the viewing. She understood that his death was a bit difficult for me—not because I liked him, but because I didn't.

"Hey, Mom."

"You'll never guess what happened?"

It could be anything—from Toto not barking at the

clients for one full day to having so many people die in the last twenty-four hours that the funeral home would actually be in the black for the first time in years. Or had my mom found a new shade of dark red lipstick? "What is it?"

"Dr. Sanchez decided to take another look at Cliff's body today. Personally, I think the sheriff might have pressured her to dig deeper."

My ego was already at an all-time low, so I had to toot my own horn. "I was the one who told her I thought Cliff might have been injected with poison."

"Oh, that's right. I forgot you were going to speak with her. Apparently, you convinced her. Seems Dr. Sanchez found some damaged cells at the injection site—a site she hadn't seen before."

I waited for the intense rush of satisfaction, but none came, mostly because I understood what it might mean to my relationship with Drake if the medical examiner reversed her decision and said Cliff had been poisoned. If the sheriff arrested Jaxson because of it, I would never forgive myself. "That's great. Did she say what kind of poison it was?"

"No, but she sent off the sample to the lab."

More waiting. More torture. "The sheriff will be busy looking for his son's killer then, huh?"

"I'm sure he will. Did Fern tell you that the funeral is scheduled for Tuesday?"

"No." I hoped Aunt Fern's memory wasn't going.

"The sheriff said he would have had it on Monday, but since that was Memorial Day, he wanted to postpone it a day. Fern said she plans on closing The Tiki Hut between one thirty until the end of the service, so you and the other staff members can attend."

"That's really nice of her."

I might have considered not going if I didn't think the

killer might show up. Sure, that probably only happened in television shows, but it was possible, nonetheless.

"Stop over tomorrow," my mom said. "I want you to take a look at my handiwork. The medical examiner tried to be neat, but a body is often not the same after a second autopsy."

I'd never noticed that, but my mother might be more sensitive to it. "Sure thing."

After we talked about how dad was doing, I hung up, determined to get this Memorial Day theme organized.

I went back to cutting the material when my cell rang. Again! I was tempted to let it go to voicemail since I didn't recognize the number. I also was tired of being interrupted. In the end, however, I caved. "Hello?"

"Glinda, this is Deputy Rocker."

My pulse skipped a beat, though I don't know why. Maybe he wanted to haul me in for being a quack. "What can I do for you, deputy?"

"I received a call from Dr. Arnold. Turns out you were right."

Whoa. I hadn't expected that. Once more, the rush of satisfaction failed to materialize though. "That's great. So, he did die from a brain bleed?"

"He did, but Dr. Arnold said the victim was to blame for his demise. Apparently, he hadn't stayed hydrated, and it was like a heat stroke. When the doctor looked further, some underlying issue in his brain caused the massive brain bleed. Besides, his doctor had told him his heart wasn't strong enough to be climbing on roofs, especially in this heat, but he did it anyway."

That was a shame. I couldn't tell if Steve was disappointed or not. I had the sense he wanted his friend to have someone to take out his anger on. "Does that mean Jake won't be suing anyone?"

"No, he won't. He says he's come to grips with the idea

that his dad was just a stubborn old man, and that was his downfall."

"Thanks for letting me know."

"Sure. I, ah, wanted to know if you would like to grab a drink sometime? My treat, of course, to thank you for giving up your free time to help me and my friend."

"There's no need." I didn't want the complication of going out on a date when my life was in chaos right now.

"It's only—" A phone rang in the background. "Hold on a sec. I'm sorry; I need to take this. It's a 911 call."

"Take it. We'll talk later." After disconnecting, I breathed a sigh of relief. It was definitely for the best that we kept our relationship professional.

I needed to take a break from all of the material cutting and grab something to eat. Penny was working today. Since I didn't want her to have to wait on me, I headed over to The Bubbling Cauldron Coffee Shop. Not only did Miriam Daniels make the best blend of coffee, she had a great array of homemade sandwiches. Of course, I would never admit that to her twin sister, Maude, who ran the Moon Bay Tea Shop, situated across the street. They were the first two shops one encountered after entering our town. As such, the elderly twins did a swift business. Both were witches, and both loved to gossip. That was maybe the best reason to stop in.

When I pushed open the shop door, the bell dangling above tinkled. Instantly, the rich coffee aroma released the tension in my body. It was as if I was entering some happy zone. I took a seat at the window and then let out a breath at the knowledge that I might survive after all.

"Glinda Goodall," Miriam said. "If this isn't a nice surprise. What can I get you, sweetie?"

"Something decadent. What with Cliff's death, Memorial

Day planning, and then Cliff's funeral coming up, I'm exhausted."

"You poor thing. I have the perfect brew. Something to eat too?"

The longer I remained at the shop, the more likely Miriam was to stop over and tell me the latest news. Between her, her twin sister, my aunt, Dolly, and Pearl, nothing escaped them.

"Yes. I'll have the hummus and cucumber sandwich."

"Perfect."

I looked out the window. Neither of the two cruisers were in front of the station, so I had to conclude that Steve was still out on his 911 call, and the sheriff was looking for clues about his son's death.

Five minutes later, Miriam carried over my coffee and my sandwich. "Here you go."

"Thanks. It looks wonderful."

"Did you hear about Floyd Paxton?" Miriam asked.

Gossip. Yes! "No." Floyd's name rarely came up in conversation. He was a curmudgeon who'd pushed around his wife one too many times—or so I'd heard. She left one day, and no one had seen or heard from her since. Miriam—and I think maybe Maude—claimed that Floyd killed her and then buried her somewhere on his large farm. "What happened?"

"Rumor has it that wolves got him. At least that was what Clarise told me. And here's the really strange part. Clarise was driving by the old farm house and noticed Floyd's front door was open."

Both Clarise and Floyd lived out of town near one another. I wonder if that was what Steve's 911 call was all about. "Finding an open door at a farmhouse doesn't seem that odd to me. It isn't as if his house is on the main thoroughfare."

"Something else must have caught her attention. Anyway, she stopped."

To snoop, most likely. "I can't imagine the horror of seeing a mauled body," I said.

"I know! At first, she thought it was a dead animal, until she noticed it was wearing clothes."

"You don't say? But how could Clarise tell he'd been killed by a wolf? I mean, he might have had a heart attack, fallen down, and then the wolves ate him."

"I thought that too, but Clarise said his body was full of bloody claw marks. If he'd already been dead, he wouldn't have bled."

I wasn't convinced, but I'd stuck my nose in too many events that were none of my business of late. I needed to stop. Except for maybe Jake's dad, things hadn't worked out when I had interfered. "I'm sure there will be an autopsy."

"I imagine," Miriam said. "You know, I never did like the old man. He came in here a few times last year but never smiled, and he acted as if he was above all of us." She lifted her chin as if to demonstrate the man's bad attitude. "My sister thought he had a soft side, but I never saw it."

"Even if he was unpleasant, I wouldn't wish death by wolves on anyone."

She pulled out the chair across from me and sat down. Since she had an assistant working the counter, I guessed she could afford to mingle.

"You are right about that. If I had been Clarise, I would have screamed and run." She huffed. "I have to say I'm a bit disappointed in her. She was careless going in alone. Who knows if the wolves were still around?"

"I totally agree." I wonder if Clarise had been the one who contacted Steve. "Did Clarise see anything else?"

"Nothing, except that the place was trashed."

I couldn't quite grasp what might have happened, but I

did love puzzles. It was my math brain. "Maybe he was a hoarder or something, and he left the place a mess."

"I don't think so. Some rooms were neat as a pin. I think she said only the living room and bedroom were torn up."

"I would have taken one look and left." It didn't matter that I would have wanted to know what prompted such devastation. "If Clarise found the door open, could Floyd have heard some howling, stepped outside, and then been attacked?" As far as I knew, no wolf could turn a doorknob.

"That was my guess, but wolves didn't wreck the place. Clarise couldn't tell if anything had been stolen though. She said she'd only been inside his house once or twice when his wife was living there."

"Do we know when Floyd died?" I didn't feel comfortable asking about the existence of blow flies. We were in an eating establishment.

Miriam leaned closer. "I think last night. It was a full moon, you know."

I had to keep from chuckling. "Are you saying you think some werewolves killed Floyd and then returned the next day to rob him?" Werewolves did not exist, nor did any other kind of shifter.

"Why not? It makes sense."

Miriam sounded so excited that I didn't want to burst her bubble. "Sure, sounds reasonable. I think Deputy Rocker might have been called in on the case. If I hear anything, I'll let you know," I said.

Miriam grinned. She acted as if I had given her the best present ever. She reached across the table and clasped my hand. "Thank you." She pushed back her chair and returned to the counter.

Once I was alone, I shook my head. Both of the Daniels sisters might be of an age where they were losing it. Did she really believe werewolves existed? It didn't matter. Right now, I just wanted to drink my coffee—which did not disappoint. The first sip did more for my mental health than sitting a few hours on the beach. For the first time in a while, I actually relaxed, partly because I didn't have to scarf down my lunch for a change.

I let my mind wander back to Floyd Paxton's demise, letting a few scenarios take root. As I was daydreaming out the window, Steve pulled up in front of the sheriff's office and parked. An idea struck. I quickly finished my coffee and sandwich, paid my bill, and then thanked Miriam before I left.

A delicious ocean breeze made the short walk to the sheriff's office delightful. Inside, Pearl was not at her desk, which I found was odd. I did spot the deputy, however. He must have heard me, because when he looked up and smiled, my heart instantly dropped into my stomach. I refused to ponder why. All I could be sure about was that I didn't want him to think I was there to discuss our possible date.

"Hey, Glinda."

"Miriam Daniels just told me something interesting," I announced.

His brows rose. "Who is Miriam Daniels?" he asked as he nodded to the chair in front of his desk.

I kept forgetting he wouldn't know all of the shop owners yet, but I thought I had mentioned them on our trip to his hometown. I pulled out the chair and sat down. "She runs the Bubbling Cauldron Coffee Shop right down the street."

"I think you told me that."

I had the sense he might be teasing me. "If you're in the mood for great tea, her twin sister, Maude, runs the Moon Bay Tea shop across the street," I added.

"I noticed those shops when I entered town. So, what did this coffee maven tell you?"

"That Floyd Paxton was killed by a wolf. Or maybe it was a werewolf."

He laughed a bit too hard. It wasn't that funny. "Werewolves?" He sobered a bit. "Has she ever seen one? I mean, I didn't know witches really existed until I met you, so maybe werewolves do exist."

I doubted that was true, but I wasn't here to get into another debate about the existence of paranormal beings. "No, but she thought that since his house was trashed, the wolf, or wolves, killed Floyd, waited until the moon was no longer full, shifted, and then entered the house."

"That's an interesting theory. I have to say that your idea about Cliff Duncan being poisoned by Oleander is a lot more plausible."

I wasn't sure if I should thank him or not, so I said nothing. "Have you seen Floyd's body?"

"I have."

"Did it look like he might have been killed by a human first, and then a wolf came in for the spoils?" I wanted to ignore the fact that Clarise said the body was bloody, implying a wolf killed him.

"That's not my place to say. Dr. Sanchez will decide."

"I imagine I'll find out the results soon then too."

He smiled. "Probably before I do. Seems the rumor mill is rather fast in this town."

Mostly thanks to his grandmother. "It is. I actually didn't come here to discuss Floyd's death, but rather I came for another reason."

"What would that be?"

"I need a quick favor."

Steve's eyes twinkled as he leaned forward. Okay, his eyes hadn't actually twinkled. It must have been the light coming in through the front door creating the illusion. "What is this favor?"

"Can you run a name through your system?"

"Like CODIS?"

That would be for criminals, and I had no idea if Greg had a record. "I'm not sure. I just need to know what kind of person a particular man is."

Steve leaned back and pressed his palms and fingertips together. "What is this about?"

"I'm not really sure, but I'm getting a rather strange vibe from a guy I met. I want to see if he's legit." Steve might think I was thinking of dating this man, but I couldn't be responsible for what conclusion he drew from my request.

He sat up and placed his fingers on his keyboard. "What is his name?"

"Greg Anderson. He lives in Morganville, Florida."

Steve typed away. He spent a good ten minutes looking. He shook his head. "The only Greg Anderson from Morganville that I found died three and a half years ago. He was seventy-seven."

"Maybe that was this man's grandfather or something."

"Could be." He spun his computer screen around.

"Or not. That man was African American. The man I'm referring to is maybe six-foot-two with pale skin, is wiry thin, and has short, bright red hair."

Steve tapped a few more keys. "I'll call the Morganville sheriff's office. I'm betting they know who he is."

If I hadn't just done Steve a favor, I probably would have suggested he not bother. But something about Greg was off. Plus, I trusted Iggy.

Steve spoke with someone in Morganville and explained the situation. He said little for much of it. "Thanks," he said.

Once he ended the call, he faced me. "Seems as if your Greg Anderson is legit, but the deputy shares your concern. The man came to town three years ago from Orange Grove, Florida. He agreed that something seemed off about him and said he'd give the other sheriff's department a call and then get back to me."

"I appreciate it. As I said, it might be nothing." Not wanting to overstay my visit, I pushed back my chair.

"You don't want to know more about Floyd?" he asked.

"Honestly? No. An animal killed him. Who broke into his house is your problem, not mine." I then smiled.

This time Steve's laugh came out more natural sounding. "I'm glad to hear you have some boundaries when it comes to snooping."

I might have been insulted if his comment hadn't held some truth. Before he had the chance to ask me out again, I thanked him and left. I only had today to finish the decorations, and I didn't want to disappoint Aunt Fern or the veterans who counted on being together at the restaurant.

CHAPTER 13

I finally finished cutting out eighteen tablecloths and a few skirts for the tables we kept along the walls. The seven white table clothes would make it an even twenty-five. Tomorrow night, a group of us would decorate the Tiki Hut, both inside and out. One of the evening servers said he'd help hang the flags on the wall. Even though Ray Zink worked the day shift, he'd volunteered to come in and help. Being a serviceman, he understood how important this coming holiday was.

At nine o'clock, I was ready to drop into bed. When my cell rang, I was hoping it was Penny, wanting to talk. I rushed into the kitchen and picked up my phone. It was Steve. I thought it was a bit late, but he might have some information for me.

"Hello?"

"It's Deputy Rocker."

After all we'd been through, he could have at least used his first name, but his formal greeting implied he considered us colleagues. Clearly, when he had invited me for a drink, it really had only been as a thank you.

"Hi."

"I received word back on that redheaded man, Greg Anderson."

I hadn't expected such prompt service. "What did you learn?"

"The deputy over in Morganville contacted someone in Orange Grove. I'm going to email you a picture. Can you tell me if this is your man?"

"Sure." I gave him my email address and then lifted the lid to my laptop. When I saw the image, my body tensed. "That's him."

"You're sure?"

"Yes, I'm positive."

"The man's real name is Victor Hilliard."

"Victor?" My pulse soared. It was highly likely that Sam's Victor was this Victor Hilliard.

"Do you know a man by that name?"

I didn't know how much to reveal. "Indirectly. What did this deputy say about him?"

"He was caught with some drugs and spent three years in prison. After serving his time, he was released. That was three and a half years ago."

I could fill in the blanks. That was when he moved and changed his name. The question was what part did Sam play in any of this? And secondly, did either one of them have anything to do with Cliff's death? I couldn't put my finger on a motive for Victor wanting Cliff gone, but I guess it depended on whether Victor changed in prison.

"I see. Thank you."

"Glinda? There's something you aren't telling me. What is it?"

I didn't know enough to accuse anyone of anything. "How about I get back to you on that? I don't want some innocent person to get caught in the middle."

"Okay, but promise me you won't investigate? You aren't trained. You don't have a license and—"

"I get it. Again, thanks. I'll see you on Tuesday for Cliff's funeral, right?"

"I'll be there, but I'll probably stop at the Tiki Hut sometime on Monday to pay my respects on Memorial Day."

"I'll see you then." I disconnected and dropped back against the sofa. Wow. Greg Anderson was most likely Victor Hillard. While Penny probably still didn't want to talk to me, I needed answers, so I called her.

The phone rang about eight times. I was about to hang up when she finally picked up. "Glinda."

O-kay, not the friendliest of greeting, but at least she answered. "We need to talk. It's about Victor, the man Sam might have been involved with back in Morganville." As soon as I said it, I realized my timeline was off. "Or maybe it was Orange Grove."

"Orange Grove?"

"Yes. Did Sam live there?"

"I don't think so."

"Hold on." I did a map search for the two cities. Turns out, they were only about fifteen miles apart, but they were in different counties. That meant Victor could have moved from Orange Grove to Morganville and changed his name with no one the wiser. "Okay. I think I found something."

I went through how Miriam told me about Floyd Paxton being mauled to death, which then gave me a good excuse to speak with Deputy Steve.

"Uh-huh. I knew it!" Suddenly, Penny's cheer had returned.

"Knew what?"

"You were looking for any excuse to see the hot deputy again."

Was that true? "No. Absolutely not. Anyway, after we

discussed whether Floyd had been killed first and then mauled, or just mauled, I asked him to find out what he could about Greg Anderson."

"Greg? As in Buffy's ex-boyfriend?"

"Yes. I never would have questioned him, but if he took out his aggression on Buffy before she came here, he might be capable of doing the same to Sam or even Cliff, though I don't know if he even knew Cliff."

"Sam isn't violent. My ex-husband might not pay his bills on time, but he never laid a hand on me or Tommy. I'm not saying Sam won't stand up for himself, because he will, but he'd never hit a woman."

I wasn't talking about hitting a woman. Whatever. "That's good to know." If Sam wasn't violent, why had Penny said she was afraid of him? Right now, that wasn't the point. "Steve called the Morganville sheriff's department. Long story short, the only Greg Anderson was a man who'd died three years ago. He was seventy-seven."

I let that sink in. "What are you saying? That Buffy's Greg isn't really Greg?"

Spelling it out might be faster. "Exactly. Deputy Rocker sent me a photo of Victor Hilliard. He is Greg. Victor was caught with some drugs, sentenced to three years in prison, and was released three and a half years ago."

Penny sucked in a breath. "Are you thinking Sam and he were partners back then? Victor was caught, but Sam wasn't?"

"You'd have to ask Sam about that. All I know is if Sam was involved in a deal gone bad and then left town on me, I'd be a bit upset," I said.

Penny didn't reply for a moment. "How would Greg, or rather Victor, learn that Sam had moved to Witch's Cove?"

"There is only one link: Buffy Bigalow."

"This is preposterous," Penny said.

"You're probably right. But let's suppose Sam and Victor had a beef with each other. It's possible Cliff found out and was somehow caught in the middle. Maybe Victor needed to silence Cliff. I know, I know, I'm just guessing here."

"Sam would never go along with any of that," Penny said.

How could she be so sure? "Fair enough. He might not have known."

"If Cliff caught the two of them planning another deal or something, Victor might have killed Cliff, but you said he was poisoned. That seems more like something a woman would do."

I laughed. "Who? Like Buffy?"

"Why not?" she asked.

Penny was grasping at straws, probably just wanting to take the heat off of her son's father. I could relate. "I don't know. I can come up with ten different scenarios, but without any facts, I'm just spinning my wheels."

"You need to tell Deputy Steve. He isn't as biased as Duncan Donut."

"That's probably true. You wouldn't mind if I suggest there might be a connection between Victor Hilliard and Sam?"

"I know Sam. He had nothing to do with Cliff's death, so go ahead."

My hands actually started to sweat. "You're sure."

"Yes."

"Okay. I'll go over to the station tomorrow. If Steve isn't there, I'll ask Pearl to ask him to meet me somewhere so we can talk. In the meantime, do you want to mention any of this to Sam to hear his side of the story?"

"How about I wait until you talk to the deputy?"

"Works for me. And Penny?"

"Yes?"

"I'm sorry I mentioned Sam's name to the sheriff," I said, assuming she had heard me.

"I know, but you were just being your OCD self."

It was the way my mind was wired. "Thank you. Talk to you tomorrow then."

"Night."

As soon as I hung up, I pulled up a blank spreadsheet on my computer. It was time to use my math skills—or rather my organizational skills—to find the answer to this mystery. In the first column, I listed everyone who might have wanted Cliff dead. Next, I had a column for motive, one for pertinent information or facts, and in the fourth column, I assigned a probability of the likelihood that this person was guilty. I then added my thoughts.

To be fair, I listed myself. I didn't have a real motive other than I thought Cliff was creepy. I did know that Oleander was a poison, though I suspect everyone who lived in Florida knew that too. I assigned a probability of ten percent to myself. I wanted to be fair.

Jaxson Harrison was next. Did he have motive? I guess. Even though it was Cliff's dad who had, in theory, framed him, Jaxson might want Cliff dead to spite the dad. If the sheriff had died, then I would have assigned a high probability to Jaxson. That last column contained my gut feelings, though I realized I might be a bit prejudice. I didn't want Jaxson to be guilty.

For the next two hours, I listed everyone I could think of. Naturally, Sam and Greg—or rather Victor—were high on my list. To keep things fair, I included Buffy, though my probability for her was low. I didn't see her as the kind who could shoot a dart at someone. That would take some skill.

Only then did it occur to me that I should have asked Dr. Sanchez if she could tell whether Cliff was stabbed with the dart—or syringe—from close range, or if the dart had been shot from a distance. While I did major in math, my grade in first year physics wasn't the best. I thought the farther the distance, the deeper the wound. Then again, I could be completely wrong.

My eyelids kept closing as I stared at the page. When I awoke, I was sprawled on the sofa, and it was four in the morning. Ugh. I had so wanted to figure this out. I guess I could work on it tomorrow—or rather later today—after I got off work. I would have liked some input from Drake, especially if we could find proof that Jaxson wasn't involved, but he might still be mad at me.

I closed my computer. I swear I'd no sooner dragged myself to bed than sunlight streamed in through the window. After I dragged myself out of bed, I surprised myself in my ability to dress and then not mess up my makeup.

As I went through the day, it took a lot of effort to smile when I took everyone's order. It had been hard—very hard.

I was never so happy when my shift was over. As much as I wanted to rush over to the sheriff's department right away and have him or Steve look into Sam Carsted, I had to trust Penny's instincts, even though she had a vested interest in keeping Sam out of jail. If she believed he wasn't a killer, I had to respect that—until I unearthed information that said otherwise.

Mad or not, I needed Drake. He was smart and logical. If we could learn who really killed Cliff, it would take the heat off his brother.

After I changed and grabbed a quick bite to eat, I gathered the fabric I'd cut so I could drop them off at Aunt Fern's apartment. She had today and only today to hem all of the tablecloths.

"Where are you going?" Iggy asked.

"To Aunt Fern's." I thought it obvious since my arms were full of material.

"Why were you up most of the night? Something is going on. Spill."

"Aren't you the curious little lizard? After I drop this stuff off at Aunt Fern's, I need to make up with Drake. After we talk, I'll fill you in on everything."

He swished his tail. "You better." He lifted his head. "Any progress on getting me a new collar?"

That seems to be all he cared about. "With the name Detective Sleuth on it?"

"I was thinking I'd like to be Sherlock Holmes-bound."

"Don't you mean Sherlock Holmes?" I asked.

"That name is taken. Since I'm more or less confined to this small town, I thought Holmes-bound would fit."

I laughed. "Because you're homebound?"

"Exactly."

"I'll think about it."

After I placed the material on Aunt Fern's sofa, I returned to my apartment, grabbed my laptop, phone, and door key, and headed out. Drake's store was closed on Sundays, but he might be working nonetheless. He did inventory at the end of every month. Before walking over, I called him, because I wasn't sure he'd even answer my knock.

"Glinda."

"Before you tell me I'm a bad friend, I really need to talk to you. Are you home or at the store?"

He hesitated for a moment. "I'm at the store."

"I'll be right over." I hung up before he could tell me not to come. Two minutes later, I knocked on his beachside door. As soon as he pulled it open, I waved my laptop. "I need help."

CHAPTER 14

After placing my computer on the counter in Drake's back room, I booted it up. "I was hoping you would take a look at this." Once it loaded, I pulled up my spreadsheet.

"That takes me back to my days in business school," Drake said, sounding none too happy.

Not everyone loved spreadsheets, but it enabled me to put a lot of information in a small amount of space. "Just look. Someone killed Cliff."

"Glinda. Seriously. I thought you weren't going to pursue this."

"I wasn't until I learned he was murdered."

"You're going with the pink crystal analysis now?" Drake asked.

"No, the medical examiner reexamined the body and found an injection site. Cliff was injected with something, and Dr. Sanchez sent the sample off to the lab to find out what it was. I didn't ask how deep the hole was, but I want to find out. It could be important."

"You do know the sheriff will probably arrest Jaxson

again?"

I shook my head. "I don't think so and here's why. I've been talking to Steve, pointing the finger in several different places. He's onboard with looking elsewhere."

"Steve?" Drake's eyebrows rose.

"Deputy Steve Rocker, and no, there is nothing going on between us so don't give me that look." I didn't feel like telling Drake that Steve had asked me out, even if it was only as a thank you for helping with his friend's father.

Drake held up his hands. "If you say so." He nodded to the spreadsheet. "I'm assuming you need a sounding board for your theories?"

"Always. I have no proof of anything, so it's not like I can knock on anyone's door and accuse them of anything."

He laughed. "Since when did that stop you?"

I punched his arm. "I'll go through my suspects and their possible motives, and you tell me what you think."

Drake said very little as I ran through the names. I explained that Buffy's boyfriend was using an alias and had served time in prison. Whether Buffy knew of her boyfriend's past or not was anyone's guess.

To my surprise, Drake didn't interrupt me when I pointed to Jaxson's name on the list but that could be because I'd listed myself too.

"I'm impressed," he said.

"Thank you. Where should we go from here?"

"You need proof. As you said, without facts you can't expect answers to your questions."

I'd already figured that much out. "Do you have a favorite suspect? I need to know where I should focus my attention."

"No one sticks out. Just because Greg Anderson aka Victor Hilliard did time does not mean he is a killer. Seems to me the guy is trying to turn his life around."

"You might be right, but why attack Sam Carsted?"

"He attacked Penny's Sam?"

We hadn't spoken in a while, so I filled him in on what Iggy said. "Penny told me about Sam's black eye and split lip from a previous altercation, but unless Sam confesses that the same man attacked him twice, we can't be positive Iggy saw this Victor guy."

"Show the image Steve sent you to your familiar."

I laughed. "Even if Iggy positively identifies him, it wouldn't hold up in court. It's not like they can swear in an iguana."

He chuckled. "No, but at least you'd know if it is this Victor from Orange Grove. I think your analysis is good, but as you said, you have no proof."

"I know. My best bet might be to talk to the five gossip queens."

He huffed out a laugh. "If anyone knows, they will."

"If I come up empty, would you mind if I show my list to Steve?"

"Not at all, but I don't think it will do much good. He can't do anything without evidence either."

"You're right. Too bad most of what I know is second hand information—and much from my familiar."

Drake cupped my shoulder and gave it a light squeeze. "You'll figure it out. You always do."

I wish I had the same level of confidence. "Thanks. I need to head back. We are decorating the Tiki Hut tonight for Memorial Day tomorrow, and I need to have everything organized and ready to go."

"I'm sure it will look great."

"I hope so for the sake of those mourning the loss of a loved one."

I left and headed back to the restaurant. For the next few hours, I put the flags and other memorabilia into individual containers and then labeled what was in each bin. Once I finished, I headed upstairs to make assignments. I wanted to hand the five helpers their bins, along with a diagram of how I envisioned the theme to be displayed.

When I stepped inside my apartment, Iggy was sitting on his stool, looking out at the ocean. "What did Drake say?" he asked without turning around.

I explained my list of suspects and their motives. "He thought my work was good, but it didn't really get us anywhere. I have no proof of anything."

"If you can get me into someone's house, I can cloak myself and gather information."

"The only information you'd get is if they called someone and confessed. Otherwise, you'd just watch someone have a drink or check out some reruns on TV." Iggy's ability to concentrate was questionable, which meant if he lost focus, he'd reappear. No telling how that person would respond. "I like your suggestion, but I need to figure out who we need to spy on first."

"You're no fun," Iggy said.

"Don't worry. You'll get your day in the sun."

He faced me—or at least his eye was looking at me. "I can get sun anytime I want."

"I meant that you will get the due you deserve when we figure out who killed Cliff."

Iggy bobbed his head, which was an act of aggression. Sometimes, he wouldn't listen to reason. Right now, I couldn't deal with him. I printed off my spreadsheet, thinking it might come in handy.

"I need to check on Aunt Fern to see how she is coming with the tablecloths," I said.

"Don't bother. She's finished."

"And you know this how?" Iggy believed he was the smartest creature in the universe.

"Because her sewing machine stopped pumping about half an hour ago."

"She might be taking a break. Aunt Fern has a touch of arthritis in her fingers, and using her hands for hours tires her. I'll be downstairs if you need me. I need to speak with Ray about something."

"About what?"

"That's none of your business." Iggy was being way too pushy, and I didn't need that right now.

Downstairs, I found Ray on the patio taking a couple's order, since he had switched shifts with the person who normally worked nights. When he finished writing up their request, I followed him back inside. "Can I ask you a military question?"

He did a double take. "A military question?"

"Yes, you must have studied weapons in the service, right?"

He chuckled. "You could say that."

"Have you ever used a blowgun?"

He stopped in the middle of the restaurant. "A blowgun?"

I didn't need him to repeat everything I said. "Yes. Let's discuss this in a more private place." I nodded to the kitchen, implying he should deliver the food request, and then we could talk. "It'll only take a minute."

After he placed his order with the kitchen, Ray returned. "Blowguns were used in the Vietnam War extensively. I never participated in that type of weaponry, but my dad did."

That wasn't ideal, but it would have to do. "Did you know that Cliff was murdered?"

"I'd heard that."

At least the rumor mill was alive and well here. "He was injected with something that killed him. The medical examiner is awaiting the lab results to learn what that might have been. My question is whether the killer was standing close to

Cliff and stabbed him with a needle, or was the killer at a distance and shot something out of a blowgun?"

Ray shook his head. "Your imagination is impressive."

What did that mean? "Look, if I can learn what the depth of the wound was or even how thick the needle puncture was, I might be able to suggest to Deputy Rocker how close the person was standing."

"Interesting. Syringes come in all thicknesses. I imagine blowgun darts would be thicker, but I'm no expert. You'd have to find the murder weapon to be certain." His brows scrunched. "Can I ask why are you getting involved? This is why we pay our law enforcement."

"I know, but I'm trying to prove that Jaxson Harrison didn't kill Cliff. Sheriff Duncan thinks Jaxson is guilty, and he isn't working fast enough to find another suspect." To be fair, I didn't know what the sheriff was thinking, but it gave me a good reason for interfering.

"Why do you think Jaxson is innocent?"

"I don't know for sure, but if I spent three years in prison, I'd use a knife or my fists to hurt someone." Oh, my, that sounded horrible. "I mean, according to what I've seen on television, men in general don't use a needle. They shoot, stab, or beat up people."

His brows rose. "You believe a woman killed a big, strong deputy based on the method of murder?"

That did sound rather ridiculous. Darn. "I don't know. I just want something plausible to suggest to the sheriff's department. They need to look deeper. Thanks for your help."

"Sure."

I spun around, and headed toward the exit. It was time to visit Deputy Steve. The medical examiner would have given him Cliff's revised autopsy report by now. Whether our newest addition to the sheriff's department would share the information with me was the big question.

Aunt Fern was still working on the tablecloths because Bertie Sidwell was at the cashier's station. She and Aunt Fern went way back. After Bertie's husband died, she was a bit lost, so my aunt suggested she work one or two days a week at the Tiki Hut whenever Aunt Fern had some errands to run. So far, it had worked out well for both of them.

Bertie was chatting with a young couple, pointing to some souvenirs in the display case, enabling me to leave unnoticed. Score! Sometimes, Bertie could talk and talk and talk.

While there weren't any cruisers in front of the sheriff's department, it was possible Steve or the sheriff had parked in back. There was only one way to find out if either of them was there—go inside.

As soon as I stepped into the station and spotted Pearl, I realized I should have picked up a few cookies for her. "Hey," I said.

She grinned. "I might have to punch your frequent visitor card." I gave her a blank look. "You know, come nine times and on the tenth visit you get a free cookie."

I laughed. "It might be worth it, as long as the cookies are chocolate chip."

She winked. "I'll be sure to stock some of those in the future."

I loved it when Pearl was in a feisty mood. Steve was at his desk, but the sheriff didn't appear to be there. "I need to discuss something with Deputy Rocker."

She grinned. "You go right ahead, hon." Pearl turned around in her seat. "Oh, Stevie. You have company."

I wasn't company, but to deny it would be rude. Our new deputy looked up and smiled. Darn it. His look was one of interest, and that was not what I wanted today. Of course, I smiled back because I needed to see the autopsy report. With an air of confidence, I strolled up to Steve's desk.

His smiled turned to a know-it-all smirk. "Are you here with more theories?"

I swallowed my snarky response. "I would think you'd be happy that I have suggestions. The medical examiner confirmed that Cliff was murdered, most likely by a poisonous dart or syringe. Don't forget that was something I suggested."

"I didn't forget."

"Good. I'm here to help."

He laughed. "I know what you're doing."

"What am I doing?" Steve did not motion I take a seat, but I figured why not relax? I pulled out the chair in front of his desk and dropped down. My back thanked me.

He placed two fingers on his temples and closed his eyes, probably trying to look like some fortune teller. "You want to see the autopsy report," he droned in an eerie voice.

Yes, I did, but he didn't need to mock me. "Why would I want to see that?" I asked with as much indifference as I could muster.

He opened his eyes and lowered his hands. "I'm not sure. You tell me."

This cat and mouse game wasn't getting me anywhere. "Fine. As I mentioned before, I believe that Cliff was poisoned with Oleander. Since he wouldn't have eaten the leaves or flowers, the only way to get it into him would be to inject it. The size of the injection site might help determine how far away the person was standing. Close implies he trusted the person. Far away means the person was lying in wait in his backyard."

"Backyard? Oh, yes, your mother had that conversation with Cliff. He said he was outside when he felt a sting."

I didn't need his overly cheerful tone at my expense—but

I did need his information. The medical examiner wouldn't share it willingly, so I had to get it some other way—namely through Steve. "Yes. Could the medical examiner tell if the person was close or far?"

"No. All she was able to determine was the depth of the wound and thickness of the needle. That wasn't enough to tell us whether it was a syringe or a dart."

Darn. So much for that line of thinking. I needed to move on. I pulled the spreadsheet I had printed out of my pocket and unfolded it. "I was doing a little thinking yesterday."

"Always dangerous."

This time, he was clearly kidding—and enjoying himself at my expense. "Anyhoo, here are my suspects and their possible motives."

I expected Steve to glance at it and then dismiss it. Instead, he actually studied it line by line. "May I keep this?"

"Sure, but I have no proof of any of it."

"I'll keep that in mind. You never know when I come across something that will corroborate your thoughts."

Not wanting to draw out this interaction any longer, I pushed back my chair and stood. "Thank you."

"Keep out of trouble, you hear? I have enough to deal with."

I hoped he was joking again. I wouldn't get into trouble, or so I believed. I left his office, no closer to finding the killer. Whoever had poisoned Cliff must be smiling, thinking he'd gotten away with something big. That, however, would be his last mistake. He didn't know Glinda Goodall.

Because the second shift was on duty when I entered the restaurant, I touched base with each of them to remind them about our decorating marathon tonight. Thankfully, everyone seemed excited. I, too, was stoked. It wasn't often that we got to hang out and chat.

Since Bertie was still at the check-out counter, I figured

Aunt Fern was either working on the decorations or taking a nap. I headed upstairs and softly knocked on her door. She answered a few seconds later. "Glinda. Did you find out something?"

I didn't know exactly what she was referring to, but ten bucks said she'd seen me exit the sheriff's department. That made sense considering her sewing machine was in her bedroom, and her sewing table overlooked the street. "Not really."

"Come in and take a load off."

"Take a load off? Have you been talking to Penny again?"

"Yes. She's teaching me the new slang, though Harold thinks I'm being silly."

"How is Uncle Harold these days?"

My aunt sighed. "He misses being alive, but he has no pain, so I'm happy for him."

"Me too. I stopped by to see if you've finished sewing the tablecloths."

She waved a hand. "I finished over an hour ago. I put them in the storage room on top of the bins."

Iggy had been right. "That's awesome. Thanks."

"What did the hot deputy have to say?" she asked in her inquisitive, gossipy tone.

I refused to give her a rundown on my suspects, because she would announce to the whole town who I suspected. "Not much." I told her that I'd wanted to find out more about the autopsy report, but what he told me didn't help.

"Iggy said you went to speak to Drake before that."

Okay, my familiar needed a stern talking to. "I did, and I think we've made up." I faked a yawn. "I'm going to take a short nap. Tonight is going to be a long one."

"You do that, dear. And thanks for helping out."

CHAPTER 15

After a very successful decorating party Sunday night, the Tiki Hut was packed for breakfast the next morning, and from all of the compliments, the decorations were a hit—as were the free meals to the military. I had no idea there would be so many who had served. Most of the customers were visitors, but that was okay. The more the merrier.

After I had taken care of my customers, I walked around to everyone's table and chatted with the diners, asking who else had served, which branch, and where? I loved hearing their stories. When I finished touching base with the people inside, I moved out to the patio.

Ray, who was working that area, came up to me. "Any news on your blowgun theory?"

"No. I told Deputy Rocker my thoughts, but the autopsy didn't really help, so we're back to square one."

"What's your plan?"

"I don't know. Cliff's funeral is tomorrow afternoon. I'm hoping the killer will show up."

He laughed. "Are you expecting him to be wearing a

sign?"

I grunted. "Of course not, but maybe he'll do something to give away his identity."

Ray's brows rose. "You've been reading too many crime stories."

Or watching too much television. "Maybe. Being curious is in my nature though. I can't help myself."

"When I pay my respects to Cliff, I'll be sure to keep a watch out for anyone suspicious."

"Thank you." Ray went off to wait on someone else, and I returned to the indoor restaurant, perhaps a bit more nervous about the funeral than before. I couldn't wait for all of this to be over.

The next day at work, as the time for the funeral neared, I reminded everyone that we would be closing soon. When the last customer left, Aunt Fern posted the Closed sign on the door indicating we would reopen after the service.

I didn't like funerals, in part because my bright pink outfits were not appropriate for church. While I didn't own anything black, I had a shift that was a very dark plum that some might mistake for black. For shoes, I had to borrow a pair from Aunt Fern since her feet were more or less my size. My mom and I wore the same size shoe, but I didn't want to bother her. She'd be busy getting everything ready. At least I wore light pink underwear to preserve my personality.

As I dashed around upstairs, I asked Iggy if he would ask Aunt Fern if I could borrow a pair of her black flats.

"I'll ask if you take me to the funeral."

I had no problem with that. Iggy had excellent hearing.

He might pick up something I missed. "As long as you stay in my handbag, you can come with me."

"Fine." He sounded way too cheerful. Something was up, and that worried me. The little devil rarely did as I asked.

He took off while I finished dressing. A knock on my front door sounded a minute later. Aunt Fern entered, holding out a pair of shoes. "You might as well keep these. You're the only one who wears them."

Having black in my closet kind of went against my creed, but I would wait to tell her that after the funeral. "Thank you."

She nodded to my combed hair. "No purple and pink hair extensions today?" she asked.

"It won't kill me to go mainstream for a few hours, but as soon as the service is over, I'm changing back."

"I figured."

My mind jumped to logistics, something I found comforting. "I can drive us to the church if you want. Parking will be at a premium though."

"I imagine so. I'm expecting most of the town to show up."

I looked at my watch. I needed to hurry. "Let me pack up Iggy and then I'll be ready. He insists on going."

"I'm right here. I can hear you." Iggy was between us.

Aunt Fern looked down at my familiar. "I have a bigger purse. I'll take him. Is that okay with you, little man?"

"Yes!" he said with too much enthusiasm.

If I had called Iggy *little man*, he would have told me in no uncertain terms that the name was unacceptable. I picked him up and handed him to her, even though our *little man* could have scaled her body in less time.

I slipped on the borrowed black shoes, and while they were a bit wide, they'd do. After I grabbed my purse, we headed out. My parents' funeral home had a chapel, but it was too small for the crowd my parents were expecting. That's why the viewing and the service would be held at the main church on the edge of town.

When we arrived, the lot was mostly full, but we managed to find a spot to park. Because I was there to spy on who came, I motioned that I was going to sit in the back.

"But Miriam and Maude are in the third row," Aunt Fern said sounding so disappointed. "Oh, and there is Pearl, right in front of them."

"You go ahead."

Aunt Fern flashed me a quick smile. "You don't mind?"

"No." I leaned closer. "I'm here to find a killer," I whispered.

"Oh! Of course. I wasn't thinking. Good luck." Aunt Fern and Iggy made their way to the front, while I sat in one of the pews in back.

I must not have been all that attentive, because Penny startled me when she slid in next to me.

Her eyes went wide, and her jaw dropped. "Wow. Black shoes, no pink hair extensions, and a dark plum dress. I almost didn't recognize you."

I chuckled softly. "I didn't think my pink Converse sneakers would be well received."

"For most of the world, sure, but everyone in this town expects it from you."

I didn't need to get into a discussion on how the town viewed me. "Is Sam coming?"

"No, he's watching Tommy."

I wanted to ask if she trusted him, but that was her business, not mine. Penny knew as much about Victor as I did, and she must have decided her former husband could take care of Tommy and deal with Victor, should he stop by. "Did you speak to Sam about his former partner?"

"I tried, but Sam was rather tight-lipped. He did say he and Victor spoke."

That was encouraging. "Did speaking involve punching, by any chance?"

"As I said, he wasn't in the mood to share, and since he was watching Tommy, I didn't want to make a scene. When I pick up Tommy after the funeral, I'll try asking again."

"Let me know if he divulges anything." I knew it was none of my business, but I couldn't help myself. I probably should research whether there was a group for my condition: TMCKTC Anonymous. That stood for: Too Much Curiosity Killed The Cat. I could be the president.

But I digress. While I'd been chatting with Penny, the church had filled up, and I needed to mentally catalog who was here. The sheriff was in the front row. Sitting next to him was Steve. Pearl sat behind those two, and my Aunt and a few of her crony friends behind them.

I leaned over at Penny. "I thought Buffy would be here since Cliff was her child's father."

"Maybe Victor told her not to come."

"That would be terrible. I would never date anyone who was that controlling."

When Penny said nothing, I had the sense that maybe Sam had been that type.

The preacher stepped up to the podium and gave a short sermon about Cliff and all the good he'd done for the community. I had to work hard to keep my expression blank. The preacher then nodded to the sheriff. When he reached the podium, he told us what a great son Cliff had been. Many people might have bought it but not me. When the sheriff had come in to eat by himself, he'd often commented about how Cliff was a screw up. Maybe death had a way of erasing the bad memories.

Only Cliff's friend, Chas Williams, went up to speak after

the sheriff. He told a few stories about how cool Cliff was and how sad it was that he'd died so young. I kept waiting for him to say what a shame it was that he never got to enjoy his son, but Chas didn't mention it. Cliff probably confided in his friend that he hadn't mentioned anything to his dad about the grandchild yet.

When the service ended, I opted not to go to the cemetery. Penny might have the day off, but I did not, and we expected a large crowd at the Tiki Hut afterward. Most of the people would want something to eat and especially drink after standing in the sun at the cemetery.

Aunt Fern spent a few minutes chatting with her friends, but since each of them had a business to run, I figured not too many planned on seeing Cliff lowered into the ground.

Aunt Fern finally made it down the aisle. "Ready?" she asked.

If there hadn't been a ton of people around, I would have asked Iggy if he'd picked up any gossip—or if Aunt Fern had.

"Yes."

As soon as I pulled out of the lot, I quizzed her. "Did any of your friends have anything to say about Cliff's death?"

"You mean who killed him?"

"Yes." I didn't think they'd be sharing a cry together.

"Maude is still waffling between Jaxson Harrison and Penny's ex-husband as being the killer."

I didn't like hearing that. "Did she give a reason?"

"No. Personally, I'm surprised Maude remembered Jaxson from when he lived here. Her memory isn't as good as it used to be."

I didn't want to say that memories from the past were sharper than ones from the present. "How about you, Mr. Iggy?"

He popped his head out of Aunt Fern's purse. "I got nothing. Your aunt wouldn't let me leave her side."

"Thank goodness for small favors," I mumbled.

Once I parked in front of the restaurant, we headed upstairs to change back into our costumes. "When I go downstairs, I'll make an extra batch of lemonade," I said, wanting to be helpful.

"That would be great. And maybe some iced tea too."

"You got it."

I was ready first, and I made it down before Aunt Fern did. After making a few extra pitchers of drinks, I made sure we had a lot of ice water on hand too. The staff seemed rather calm until the hoards descended upon us. I stayed to help out the second shift, until the crowd thinned.

After doing my usual checkout routine, I headed upstairs once more. I'd just entered my apartment when a knock sounded on my door. It wouldn't be Drake since he was working today. It was his stated reason for not going to the service, but I knew the real reason—he didn't like Cliff—and I didn't blame him one bit.

My visitor wasn't Aunt Fern because she was at the cash register downstairs.

"Coming," I called.

When I opened up the door, I was surprised to find Penny. Her gaze bounced every which way, and she was shifting from foot to foot. My best friend rushed in. "I think Sam killed Cliff."

My breath totally left me, and my heart jammed against my ribcage. "You think Sam killed Cliff? Let's not jump to conclusions. Sit down, and I'll get you something to drink. We can figure this out."

"Just water. I need to think."

"Where's Tommy?" I asked.

"He's downstairs. Your aunt is watching him."

This must be serious. Bringing Tommy here was a last resort. While Aunt Fern loved to babysit, she fed Tommy so many cookies that Penny said it was difficult to bring him down from the sugar high after they got home.

"Tell me what happened?" I said as I handed her a glass of water.

"After the funeral, I went to pick up Tommy. When he and I moved out of the house, I didn't think to pick up my nice gardening tools."

Sam's grandfather had left him that house when he passed, so it made sense that Penny would be the one to move out. "I remembered you said you liked to garden when you lived there."

She sniffled. "I did. Anyway, Tommy was playing quietly in the living room when I got there, so I went out back to the shed. Even though I'd lived there for years, I must not have been paying attention back then, because that is when I saw it."

Penny liked to drag out a story. "Saw what?"

"The Oleander bush."

Was that what this was about? "Penny, those bushes are everywhere."

"I know, which was why I continued on into the shed." She pulled out her cell phone, located a picture and showed it to me. "This is what I found."

I shook my head. "It's a mortar and pestle. We use those in the kitchen to grind up spices and such." Reality dawned. "Oh, frack. Are you thinking Sam used it to grind up some Oleander?"

"Maybe."

"Did it smell sweet? Some Oleander flowers are quite fragrant."

"I didn't smell it. I didn't want to get sick."

Questions bombarded me. "We need to tell Steve. I mean Deputy Rocker. He could test the mortar and pestle for traces of Oleander. I can't think of any reasons why someone would grind up the leaves unless it was to make something lethal."

When Penny didn't even react to that slip about Steve, it meant she was in a bad head space right now. "I don't know. I don't want my child to lose his father."

She wasn't making sense. "You don't want Tommy around a killer, do you?"

"Sam didn't kill anyone."

"Whoa! Weren't you the woman who rushed into my apartment and announced Sam might have killed Cliff a moment ago?"

"I know, but telling you all of this has changed my mind. I think Sam must have been framed. I wouldn't have married a killer. He might have abused drugs, drank too much, or gotten into some fights, but he's no killer. I never would have hooked up with him if he had been that bad." Penny's hands shook and tears brimmed on her lids.

I wanted to believe her, but she was acting a little unstable. I tried to figure out how the mortar and pestle might have gotten into Sam's shed without his notice. "We can work through this. If you didn't smell the stuff in the mortar, you can't be sure it is Oleander, can you?"

Penny sniffled. "I guess not."

"Did you say anything to Sam about what you found?"

"No! I grabbed my trowel, work gloves, watering can, and a few other things, and walked back in. I casually grabbed Tommy and left. Then I came here."

"Smart."

I put on my detective hat. "If Sam had been framed, his fingerprints wouldn't be on either the mortar or the pestle. If he did use it, he might have needed to grind up drugs or something. That would explain why it was there. But if he used it to grind up Oleander, he would have gotten rid of the evidence, right?"

"Probably. I think Sam is a smart guy and all," Penny said. "Even if it was Oleander, I don't think he'd know how to liquify it. Wouldn't that take some doing? Like cooking it or something?"

"How would I know?" Okay, I had minored in chemistry, but I'd never extracted liquid from a leaf. "We can't just sit here and pretend you never found it. That would make us accessories if Sam is caught and found guilty."

Penny's shoulders slumped. "You're right. Do you think anyone is at the sheriff's department now?"

"It's kind of late. Pearl would have gone home, but Jennifer Larson might be there. The sheriff wouldn't want the office unattended."

Penny stood. "Let's go."

CHAPTER 16

Both Jennifer and Steve were in the office when Penny and I walked in.

Jennifer looked up from the reception desk. "Glinda. Penny. How can I help you?"

"I have some evidence about Cliff's murder that I need to share with your deputy," I said.

Jennifer's eyes widened. "By all means. Go on back."

Penny and I went over to his desk. Steve didn't look surprised to see us, and I worried I was becoming a pest.

"Ladies. How can I help you?" Thankfully, he sounded pleasant instead of annoyed.

I dragged over a second chair from against the wall. Once we were seated, I motioned with my eyes to Penny's phone.

She turned to me. "I don't know if I can do this."

"You have to. It could be important. Go on and show the deputy."

She turned on her phone, brought up the picture, and handed it to Steve. He studied it for a few seconds. "What am I looking at?" he asked.

Penny gave him the rundown about seeing the Oleander

bush in Sam's backyard and then finding this in the shed. "I don't even know if it had Oleander in it, but if it did, I'm sure my ex-husband wouldn't have killed Cliff. I think he is being framed. I want you to find out who would do this."

"I'll try," was all Steve said.

Penny looked over at me, her chin wobbling. This was unraveling fast. "Maybe you can get a search warrant and then test the substance for ground up Oleander," I said.

"The problem is that it isn't against the law to grind up flowers," Steve said.

"True, but if there are fingerprints on it that don't belong to Sam, it might point to the killer."

Steve looked at Penny. "Tell me this. Do you think ground up Oleander leaves would fit in a syringe?"

"Probably not."

He must think we were two dumb women. I needed to step in. "I'm sure you'd need some kind of centrifuge to liquify the plant substance once it was ground up."

He turned back to Penny. "Would your ex-husband have access to such equipment?"

"No, which is why I don't think he killed anyone, but I wanted to show you this in case you think he's guilty. He and Cliff did not like each other."

"Neither did Glinda, according to her spreadsheet."

Me and my analysis.

"What spreadsheet?" Penny asked me.

I was in trouble now. "I'll tell you later. What about that Victor guy? He didn't like Sam. Maybe he killed Cliff and planted the evidence on Sam to get back at him for something."

One of Steve's eyebrows rose. "That is a reach. I'd need evidence."

That was something I didn't have. Think. Think. I turned to Penny. "Where did you find the mortar and pestle? Was it hidden, which meant you needed to move something so you could take a picture of it, or was it in plain sight?"

"In plain sight."

No one would believe Sam was a murderer by that alone, but shy of asking him about it, I needed something else. I snapped my fingers. "You didn't happen to see a syringe, Penny, did you?"

Her mouth opened and her chin jutted forward. "Of course not. Don't you think I would have taken a picture of that too?"

She took pictures of everything. "Yes, you would have."

"Penny, send me the photo, okay?" He wrote down his email address. "I'll see if I can get a warrant for a search. If I can't, I'll just ask Sam directly if I can check his shed. If he is innocent, he won't mind."

"I'm hoping he won't," Penny said. "But look for a syringe just in case. If it's not there, maybe look around Cliff's house. Whoever is framing Sam needs to be caught."

His cell rang. "I will look into it," he said before answering his phone.

That was their cue to leave.

After we met with Steve, Penny gathered up her son and left. I wanted to do something to help my friend, but I didn't know what. Assuming Steve would follow up, I had to let it go. The ball was in his court now.

I trudged up the stairs and went into my apartment. Without any prompting on Iggy's part, I told him everything. I think I just wanted to talk it out so I'd know in my heart that I'd done all I could.

"I'm not so sure Sam didn't kill Cliff," Iggy said.

"Why is that?" Usually Iggy was spot on, but this time I wasn't convinced.

"I don't know. Call it iguana gut intuition."

"I hope you're wrong. It would be hard on Penny to raise a kid on her own. She relies on Sam to pick Tommy up from school since he works an early morning shift."

"Let's hear what Steve has to say first. Then we can decide our next move," my sassy iguana said.

We? "Did the deputy hire you to take the lead on this case?" I asked.

Iggy swung around, closed his eyes, and stretched out on the stool by the window. His passive aggressive behavior was getting worse.

Even though it wasn't all that late, I fixed a quick meal, showered, and then crawled into bed to read. Perhaps if I stopped focusing on this case, something would occur to me.

But did it? No. I read one chapter of a new book and promptly fell asleep. Way before I was ready to rise and shine, my alarm went off, jarring me out of a deep sleep. I slapped the clock to shut off the annoying noise and grunted when I realized it was indeed morning, and that I had offered to cover for Corinne today. Ugh. I hated getting up early, but that was the price I had to pay for having the first shift.

I cleaned up, ate a quick breakfast, and headed downstairs. It wasn't until about eleven that things got busy. Then around noon, Pearl waltzed in and ordered two lunches to go. "I'll put the order in now," I told her.

After I turned the request in to the kitchen, I went back to Pearl, who was now chatting with Aunt Fern. Energy was swirling around those two. It must be gossip time!

I sidled up to Steve's grandmother. "How is the sheriff doing?" I asked.

"He took the day off in part because the mayor told him

to let Steve work the case. He said Bill's involvement was a conflict of interest."

About time the mayor realized that. "Good. The sheriff probably isn't in the best frame of mine to work anyway."

"No, which is why I'm worried about him. Grief can destroy a person." She turned to my aunt. "Right, Fern?"

"Absolutely."

As much as this bonding time was nice, I wanted to know if Steve had managed to get a judge to give him a warrant for Sam's shed. "Does the deputy have any leads?" I asked, trying to sound as innocent as possible.

Pearl wagged a finger at me. "You don't fool me. I heard about the mortar and pestle found at Penny's old house."

And here I thought Steve was discreet. "Do you have bugs in the sheriff's office or something?" Her face turned pinker than my Converse sneakers. "You sly dog, you. What else did you hear?"

She glanced around, probably to see if she had an audience. "Just that Steve called Sam and asked if he could stop by."

That sounded promising. Just then the chef called my name. "Your food is up, Pearl." Darn. "I'll be right back."

I grabbed the To-Go meals and handed them to her. "I hope Steve finds something and quick."

"Me too."

As soon as Pearl left, Penny rushed up to me and asked if I'd heard from Steve. "He's not my boyfriend or anything," I said. "I don't expect him to call me with what he's found out either. I'm sure the deputy has a code of ethics."

"He has to know how important this is to you since we are friends."

Seeing Penny's pain hurt me. I rubbed her arm. If it had been Drake involved in something shady, I'd be just as neurotic.

"He knows how close we are," I said.

"This is so frustrating."

"Stop worrying. Steve will figure out the truth, I'll hear about it, and then I promise you'll be the first person I tell."

"Thanks." Penny's cell rang, and she stiffened.

Penny checked the caller I.D., and then answered. A moment later, she turned and walked toward the hallway for more privacy. I took an order for my table, and when I entered the hallway that led to the kitchen to drop it off, Penny was no longer on the phone. Instead, she was leaning against the wall, her chest caved in, and tears streaking down her cheeks. My heart nearly stopped.

I rushed over to her. "Penny, what is it?"

She opened her eyes. "I can't believe it. It's wrong, that's what it is."

"What's wrong?"

"Steve arrested Sam."

"What?"

Penny looked like she was about to collapse, so I guided her over to the staircase that led to my apartment and made her sit down. "Tell me everything."

"I don't know much. Sam called to say he was in jail and couldn't pick up Tommy from school today."

"He'd only do that if the mortar and pestle had Oleander in it as well as Sam's fingerprints. Even then, the evidence is slim. Unless Steve found the syringe too."

"I don't think so. Sam swears he didn't know anything about any mortar and pestle. He said he never even owned one, and I believe him. People usually use one in the kitchen. Sam is a beer and pizza kind of guy, not some chef."

A chef wouldn't keep it in a shed. "I'm sure Steve is being cautious. He found what he believes might have been used in a crime. He had to arrest Sam."

"What am I going to do?"

"You pick up Tommy today. I'll take your tables for the last hour."

Penny hugged me. "You are the best friend a girl could have."

"You would do the same for me. And don't worry. Everything is going to be fine." That was probably a lie, but it seemed to be what Penny needed to hear.

"Thank you." She stood, wiped the moisture from under her eyes, and headed back toward the bathroom, probably to wash her face.

When I reentered the restaurant after turning in my order, I swear it looked like another tour bus had arrived. For the next two hours, we were crazy busy. I probably didn't do the best job either, because my mind couldn't keep away from Sam's arrest. I was certain Penny was blaming herself for it. All I could hope for was that the real killer would let down his guard and say something to incriminate himself. Okay, okay. I was desperate.

By the time my shift was up, I needed a calm, rational person to talk to, so I called Drake.

"Hey, what's up?" he asked.

"Sam was arrested."

"What?"

"That was my reaction. We have so much to catch up on. Can you meet me at Maude's Tea Shop in ten minutes?" Drake wasn't much of a coffee guy, and I didn't want to stay at the Tiki Hut for obvious reasons.

"Sure can."

"Thank you."

Not wanting anyone to ask me to do something else, I dropped my crown off at my apartment, changed out of my costume, and then slipped out the side entrance before heading one block north to the tea shop. I arrived before Drake, so I grabbed us a table. I hoped that of all days, the five gossip queens would be connected, and I'd learn something important.

Drake rushed in and sat across from me. "Tell me everything."

He hadn't been to the funeral, so I gave him a rundown of the service. I told him what Penny had found in Sam's shed, and how we turned over that tidbit of information to Steve. "Steve must have gone to Sam's house, asked to check his shed, and found the mortar and pestle."

"First off, if Sam had murdered Cliff, why wouldn't he have tossed the incriminating evidence somewhere else?"

"That's what I was wondering too. All I can think of is that he didn't expect anyone to search the shed."

"Then why agree to let Steve look?" Drake asked.

"Good question."

"Did they find a syringe?"

"Not as far as I know, but maybe Steve is still looking," I said.

Maude came over and smiled. "This is a nice surprise."

I didn't know why. We came here most Wednesdays. I ordered my usual sweet tea, which was a mixture of green and black tea, whereas Drake had a peach oolong with a touch of Moroccan Mint. Drake was such a tea connoisseur.

"Any sweets?" Maude asked.

The longer we stayed, the more likely it was for her to share some good gossip. "I'll have a cranberry muffin."

Drake held up a hand and then patted his already flat stomach. "Nothing for me, thanks."

I had to laugh. Men and their bodies.

Three minutes later, Maude returned. "I didn't see you at the service, young man."

"I had a shop to run."

"Uh-huh. So did we all."

I needed to find out if she knew anything. "Do you or your friends have a theory about who killed Cliff?"

She checked to see if anyone was near and then moved closer. "At first, I thought it was Sam Carsted, but then I remembered something after the funeral."

My pulse soared. "What would that be?"

"Well, the night before Cliff was found dead, I was watching a rerun of *Murder She Wrote* on television. It's such a shame they don't make them anymore."

"I think Angela Lansbury might have had enough of the show."

"Maybe. Anyway, I finished the show around nine when I heard a car door close across the street. You do know Cliff lived across from me?"

"Yes. It helped you feel safe."

"It did. Of course, I had to look out the window to check it out."

"Naturally," Drake chimed in. From the slight smile on his face, he was enjoying her trip down memory lane.

"What did you see?" I asked, wanting her to get to the point.

CHAPTER 17

"I saw a young woman getting out of a black RAV4 and enter Cliff's house," Maude said.

"How did she enter?" I asked, putting on my non-authorized detective's hat. "Did she go through the front door or sneak in through the window?"

"Why she knocked, of course."

My question hadn't been that dumb. "Are you sure it was a RAV4?" Most elderly women weren't that astute when it came to identifying the make and model of a car, especially at night.

"Yes, I'm sure. My grandson just bought one."

That worked for me. "Did you recognize this woman?"

"No, but she was about my height and had light blonde hair, hair even lighter than yours."

Mine was quite pale. There was only one person I could think of who fit the bill: Buffy Bigalow. "How long did she stay?"

"Not long. I poured myself a cup of tea, and when I came back to check, her car was gone."

Boiling water only took a few minutes. That implied

Buffy might have only been there for five minutes. "Was anyone with her?"

"Not that I saw, but that's not to say someone wasn't in the passenger seat. It was dark. Did I mention that?"

"Yes, you did." Poor Maude. Her memory was going. "Did you tell all of this to the sheriff?"

"To be honest, I was so stunned by Cliff's death that I forgot all about her. I think he only asked if I'd seen anyone that morning, and I hadn't. I'm really sorry."

"That's okay."

Maude's brows pinched as she glanced from me to Drake and then back at me. "Do you know who she might have been?"

"I'm guessing Buffy Bigalow."

"Who?"

I couldn't believe Maude didn't know her. "She's the woman Cliff had a baby with."

Her hand went to her heart, and for a moment I feared she might collapse. Drake shot to his feet and pulled out a chair. "Sit down."

Maude did. "Cliff has a child?"

Oh, boy. I'd stepped in it now. "So she claims. His name is Dusty, and he's three and a half years old." After my faux pas, I had to give her the rundown. "Buffy told us that once Cliff had learned she was pregnant, he told her to leave town. But...according to his friend Chas—the one who spoke at the service—it was Buffy who had just up and left without saying anything to Cliff."

"This is shocking. Does the sheriff know?"

"Not to my knowledge, but who's to say. He might now. It wasn't something I wanted to mention to him."

While I really appreciated Maude's intel, it didn't mean Buffy had harmed Cliff. Most likely she'd gone to his house to beg him not to ask for custody. I had to admit, I didn't think she had it in her to be so forward. The last time she and Cliff had conversed—or rather the first time—Cliff had hit her. Again—that was what Buffy said.

Maude inhaled, pushed back her chair, and stood. "I see I need to chat with Pearl. She's been holding out on me."

"You do that." As soon as she was out of earshot, I turned back to Drake. "What do you think?"

"I'm more confused than ever."

My cell rang. I thought it might be Penny, but instead it was Steve. I turned the screen toward Drake, so he'd know. "Hey, Steve."

"You were right."

I never expected to hear that confession from him. "About what?"

"Oleander was the cause of death."

Score one for me. I couldn't help but smile. "I take it the medical examiner received the lab results back?"

"Yes. That meant I had to arrest Sam. You knew that, right?"

"I did. Penny told me." I wasn't going to ask him his reasons. After all, we had practically handed him the case.

"You and I both know that finding the mortar and pestle is in no way enough evidence to prosecute Sam."

My pulse sped up. "Then why arrest him?" I was trying to keep my voice down, but my emotions were getting the best of me.

"Are you free to stop by the station? We need to talk."

I did a mental fist pump. "I'm with Drake right now. I trust him implicitly. Can he come?"

"Who's Drake?"

I explained that he was one of my best friends, not that he was Jaxson Harrison's brother. "He also owns the wine and cheese shop across the street from you."

"If you can assure me he won't blab to anyone, he can."

"He won't say anything. I promise. We'll be right over." I sounded like a school girl.

It had probably been unwise of Steve to trust me, but I wasn't going to question it.

"What was that about?" Drake asked.

"Steve wants us to stop by the station. He has some important information for me." That was a guess on my part, but I didn't want Drake to say he didn't want to come.

He pulled out his wallet and extracted his credit card. He'd paid the last time we were here, so it was my turn, but he was halfway to the counter before I could say anything. I finished my muffin, gathered my purse, and waited for Drake.

"Let's see what the deputy has to say," Drake said once he returned.

I had to admit I was a bit nervous. I wanted Steve to tell me he'd found additional evidence to prove Sam was innocent, but if Steve arrested Sam, that wouldn't be the case.

We crossed the street, and when we entered the station, Pearl looked up, but she didn't smile this time. "Steve is expecting you in the conference room."

Her stern greeting had me curious, but I had other things to worry about right now. Steve was waiting in the conference room. He needed a shave and a fresh uniform, implying he'd had a real rough day. In front of him was a steaming cup of coffee and a folder. He looked up and motioned we take a seat. I introduced the two of them, and they shook hands.

"Thanks for coming. This is sensitive information, so please keep this between us."

That sounded so ominous. "Okay," I said.

"I went to Sam's house. He was very accommodating when I asked to check his shed. Sure enough, I found the mortar and pestle in the same spot as when Penny was there."

"So you arrested him for that?"

Steve interlaced his fingers and leaned back. "Here's the thing. After looking around Sam's shed and hearing his story of his interaction with Victor Hilliard, my gut told me Sam was being framed."

"That's great. Why arrest him then?" None of this was making any sense.

"I wanted everyone to believe that the police thought Sam was guilty."

I glanced over at Drake, and from the way his lips were pulled back into a thin line, he didn't understand it anymore that I did. "What are you saying?" I asked.

"I asked Sam to come with me to the station to make the killer think he was in the clear. Sam is safe here. I then searched the exterior of Cliff's house for the syringe. The weekly trash hadn't been picked up."

"Did you find anything?" I asked.

"I did. When I went through Cliff's trash—which is something I wouldn't wish on anyone—I found the syringe."

"That's fantastic." This was the first piece of real evidence.

"I sent it off to the lab to check for fingerprints. I dusted the mortar and pestle myself for prints but found none. That would be consistent with someone framing Sam."

Drake leaned forward. "Let me get this straight. Do you really think the killer would have wiped clean the mortar and pestle but not the syringe that was used to murder someone?"

"It's possible something startled the killer. Maybe he didn't have time to wipe it clean before he tossed it in the trash."

That was a stretch. "When will you get the results?" I asked.

"They promised to put a rush on it. Murder evidence goes to the top of the pecking order, so hopefully by tomorrow."

I had no idea where this lab was located, just that it wasn't in Witch's Cove. "What can we do to help?"

"Tell me where Buffy and Victor are staying."

I figured he'd point a finger at Victor sooner or later. Sam believed he was the only one who would want to frame him. I somehow doubted Sam would have revealed why those two disliked each other, but I was betting it had to do with either money or ratting Victor out during some crime.

I told him they were staying in the apartment above the fabric store on the edge of town. Victor's prints were already in the system, so once the fingerprints came back, it would be easy to compare them to his.

"Thanks. My main concern is that if you hear about Sam being the murderer, you need to go along with it. You can't start listing all of the reasons why he's innocent."

So that was why he needed me. I was the blabbermouth. "Sure, but the biggest threats to any leaks are your grandmother, Miriam and Maude Daniels, my aunt, and Dolly Andrews."

"I might only have recently been deputized, but from all my visits to my grandmother, as well as your detailed rundown the other day, I'd figured that was so. It's why we are in this sound proof room. I'm sure this is killing my grandmother not to hear our every word, but it can't be helped."

That might have been the reason for her sour expression. I was going to suggest they hire a different receptionist, but that would destroy Pearl. "I get it. I'm to go about my business as usual. My only concern is keeping this bit of news from Penny. Just so you know, she is a witch and can tell every time I'm lying."

"Put on your game face. If the evidence I find proves Sam innocent as I suspect, she'll have her ex-husband safe and sound in a few days. Can you last that long?"

That would be hard. "I'll try."

THE NEXT TWO days were the longest of my life. Penny was a basket case, and I could understand why. She and Sam might be divorced, and they didn't get along most of the time, but she did rely on him to help out with Tommy. I suspected she was just scared of truly being a single mom. I wanted to tell her what was going on more than anything, but I honestly didn't trust her not to leak the information to someone—and that someone could be the killer.

I called Drake that night after I got off work, but just as we were in the middle of our discussion, a customer came into his store. That was totally frustrating. Sure, I could have talked to Aunt Fern, but the whole *keep-this-to-yourself* mandate would be violated. That was why I made sure to sequester myself in my bathroom when I spoke to Drake. I couldn't afford to have Iggy hear anything either. This cone of silence was pure torture.

It was around twelve-thirty on day two when Steve called. My heart pounded as I fumbled to get my phone out of my pocket. Of course, I was chatting with Penny at the time.

"Who's that?" she asked.

"Steve." I purposefully only used his first name so she'd focus on something personal rather than wondering why the deputy would be calling.

"Ooh. To ask you out?"

Really? Why not ask if it was about her ex-husband? I pretended to be star struck in order to keep this farce up a bit longer. When she learned the truth, she might never forgive me. "Maybe."

Not wanting Steve to hang up, I answered, rushed down the hallway, and went halfway up the steps to my apartment before I spoke. "Hey. Did you get the results you were expecting?" The cheer in my voice was undeniable, because I was positive he'd tell me some good news.

"As a matter of fact, yes. "

"Victor killed Cliff, right?" I kept my voice as soft as possible.

"It appears so. I'm about to pick him up now."

"That's great. I hope he's still in town. But if I was a killer, I certainly wouldn't be sticking around afterward," I said.

"It's why I need to hurry. Once more, I'm going to ask you to keep a lid on this."

While Victor hadn't had his day in court, it seemed like a slam dunk to me. "Okay. Sam is guilty until you drag Victor in, right?"

"Right. And thanks."

He disconnected. Part of me was excited that justice was about to be served, yet I also dreaded keeping my trap shut for a few more hours. As I headed down the steps, it occurred to me that Victor's motive for killing Cliff was suspect. If his goal was to frame Sam because of some slight, why not just kill Sam? Victor had probably never met Cliff before he came to get Buffy. Or had he?

Before Penny came looking for me, I hightailed it back to the restaurant. My friend was busy, so I checked on my tables. After avoiding Penny for the next two hours, I finally caught her alone. "If you need to pick up Tommy, I can finish covering your tables."

"Thanks, but my mom has grandmother duty today. When I get off work, I'm going to check on Sam. I can't imagine what he's going through. Being held in that stinky place has to be traumatic."

"Do you really want to chat with a killer?" I had to work hard to say those words.

She huffed. "Sam is innocent until proven guilty, and as far as I can tell, our deputy doesn't have a lot to go on. Do you know if he even tested the mortar and pestle for Oleander yet?"

I wanted to tell the truth as much as possible. "Yes. There was Oleander in there."

"And you didn't tell me?"

The quick sand was sucking me lower. "I thought I had." Lies. Lies. And more lies.

"You know you didn't, but we'll talk about that later. Were there any fingerprints?"

Once more, the truth seemed to be the best course of action. "It was wiped clean."

"Something seems off."

That was because it was. As if the gods of good timing were looking down on me once more, the chef called my name. I smiled. "To be continued."

I rushed off and picked up my meal for table four. I fully expected to hear back from Steve, announcing the case was all wrapped up, but he didn't call. As tempted as I was to contact him, it wasn't my place. My original goal was to make sure that Jaxson wasn't falsely accused of the crime. To that end, I had succeeded.

CHAPTER 18

I was serving a couple from Connecticut when I happened to glance out the street side window and froze. I never expected to see Duncan Donut and Steve Rocker escorting Buffy Bigalow in handcuffs into the station. For one, I didn't think the sheriff was supposed to be involved in the case anymore. Then again, I shouldn't be surprised. The sheriff was the type to do whatever he wanted.

At least, I didn't see Dusty. No mother would want her child to witness an arrest. If Victor Hilliard killed Cliff, why arrest Buffy though? Was she an accomplice?

I told myself it didn't matter. Cliff's murder was none of my business. Still, I wanted to find out what was going on. I hurried over to Penny. "I need a favor."

"Anything."

"Can you cover for me for the next few minutes?" Our shift would be over by then.

"Sure," she said. "What's going on?"

"Do you trust me?" That was a corny thing to say, but it would take too long to explain everything, especially the part about Sam not really being a suspect.

"Of course."

Not wanting Aunt Fern to question me either, I untied my apron, set it on the staircase to my apartment, and rushed out the back way. If my aunt had seen me, it wouldn't have been so easy to get away. I dashed across the street and barged into the sheriff's department where Buffy was struggling against her restraints.

She looked over her shoulder at me. "Oh, Glinda. Thank goodness, you're here. You have to help me."

"Is Dusty okay?" It was the only thing I could think of to ask.

"Yes. Some woman is watching him."

"My neighbor is keeping an eye on him," Duncan Donut said as he kept a hand on her arm.

"I thought you suspected Victor of killing Cliff." I addressed my comment to both men. I probably shouldn't have said that out loud, but my mouth often moved faster than my brain.

"It's a long story," Steve said. "Go back to the restaurant, Glinda." He gave me a stern look.

Maybe this was another one of his tricks. He had that fearful look that implied I'd mess up another one of his sting operations if I didn't. He might have arrested Buffy in order to trick her into ratting out Victor in order to save herself. Yes, I know. I watched too many television shows.

"Okay, but..." I was going to say call me so we could talk, but he owed me nothing. "Never mind."

I spun on my heels and raced out. I didn't stay long enough to find out what happened to Sam. This whole thing was so frustrating that it was causing me a lot of stress. A normal person would swear off finding justice and be satisfied with working full time, but not me. That wasn't who I was.

I approached the side entrance and planted my back

against the outside wall. I needed a moment to think. I had to tell Penny about Sam, but only if she promised to not say anything for a bit. Steve was sure to give me the all clear now that he had Buffy in custody.

After I spent a few minutes clearing my head, I slipped inside. Even though our shift had just ended, I decided to help refill the condiments first before clocking out.

I stepped into the restaurant, waved to Penny, and then went through the motions of cleaning up the side table.

A few minutes later, she rushed over to me. "Glinda, where did you go?"

"I needed to talk to Steve."

"Why? Did something happen to Sam?"

I had to tell her. "I saw Duncan Donut and Deputy Rocker escort Buffy into the station—in handcuffs."

She sucked in a breath. "Buffy? Why?"

I thought it was obvious, but maybe something was going on that I wasn't aware of. "If I had to hazard a guess, it was because Steve suspects her of having something to do with Cliff's death."

Her eyes widened. "Then they're letting Sam go?"

I opened my mouth to spill the beans when someone answered for me.

"Actually, she killed him." We both turned and found Sam standing there with a grin on his face.

I definitely didn't expect Penny to run to him and give him a hug. Considering they had been married, I guess it made some sense. Kind of. Or not. Thankfully, there was no smooching. If he had been released, he should know something.

"What do you know?" I asked, guiding us down the hallway for more privacy.

"I'm not sure how much Steve revealed to you, but while

the mortar and pestle found in my shed was used to make the serum that killed Cliff, the prints were wiped clean."

"He told me that much, but how does that prove Buffy killed Cliff?"

"The deputy found the syringe that killed Cliff in the trash behind his house. After it was tested for contents and fingerprints, they found Victor's fingerprints on it."

That was what Steve had implied. "Which would mean Victor killed Cliff and not Buffy." I must have been having a brain fart today, because I couldn't follow everything.

"That's the thing. Buffy's prints were on it also."

They were? And Steve didn't tell me? To be honest, that might have been smart on his part. "Wow."

"Are they arresting him too?" Penny asked.

"Yes. Deputy Rocker is on his way to do that now."

"I can't believe you're free," Penny said, grabbing a hold of his shoulders and running her gaze up and down his body.

"Me too." He looked over at me. "Did you know that Buffy was a nurse's aide in Morganville?"

"That I didn't know." I should have checked her out more thoroughly. That was my fault for overlooking her as a possible suspect. I had been taken in by her innocent attitude. She'd even passed Penny's lie detection test, which was even more scary.

"Buffy came to Witch's Cove because she had been offered a job at the hospital as a nurse's aide."

"She didn't mention that," Penny finally said.

"I can see why," I said, interrupting Sam's telling of the story. "She might have come here for the express purpose of killing Cliff if he tried to take Dusty away. By working at a hospital, she'd have access to the equipment needed to turn the Oleander leaves into a liquid."

"It's possible," Sam said. "I couldn't hear everything, but

apparently, Buffy went over to Cliff's house the night he was killed to ask him to drop his request for shared custody."

It didn't take a genius to figure out what he said. "I'm guessing he said no."

"Buffy was yelling so much, I was having a hard time putting all of the pieces together, but from what I could tell, she came prepared with a syringe full of poison in case he refused to drop his request. She claimed she didn't have a choice. Dusty was her child, and Cliff wasn't fit to be a father—or so she said. Buffy claimed that she only wanted to make him sick, but he died instead."

"People always have a choice about whether to do the right thing or not. I'm not sure how she figured out Cliff was unfit since she'd only been here a week or so," I added.

"Maybe she had a sixth sense. Cliff was a creep," Penny said.

"Good point. How did Duncan Donut take the news that he was a grandfather?"

"His face turned the color of sand, and I swear he was going to have a stroke," Sam said.

"Poor Duncan Donut."

"Poor Cliff," Sam said.

Even though Buffy was a pretty woman, and Greg, or should I say Victor, wouldn't be on any male model calendar any time soon, he didn't strike me as the type to do anything for Buffy. "I trust she convinced Victor to get rid of the murder weapon?"

"Yep, and good old Victor decided to kill two birds with one stone."

"By framing you?" Penny asked.

"Uh-huh."

"Why did he hate you so much?" Penny asked.

"Penny, I'm tired. We'll have to save that very long conversation for another time."

Penny's lips pressed together. That wouldn't be a conversation I wanted any part of. "Now what?" I asked. "You're in the clear, right?"

"I am."

"I'm glad Victor will be arrested," I said.

"He needs to be. Victor covered up a crime. According to Buffy, he was in on it. If I understood what was being said over her shouts, Victor wanted to help raise Dusty as his own, and Buffy wanted that too."

I finished the train of thought. "When Cliff didn't go along with that, she and Victor probably concocted a plan to kill him."

"I don't know how much of it was planned, but that sounds right. I'm happy Victor will be out of the way for a long time."

Penny smiled. "Me too."

"Thanks for the update." If I had more questions, I could ask Steve when things settled down.

"Do you want to see Tommy?" Penny asked Sam.

His grin said it all. I wasn't sure how I felt about this change in their relationship, but for once I was going to keep my mouth shut.

It took about four days for this new development in Cliff Duncan's murder to calm down. To be honest, I was kind of sick and tired of hearing about it. Aunt Fern had extracted some additional details from Pearl, but nothing that would affect the outcome. The trial was set for three weeks from now. According to Pearl, to reduce his sentence, Victor basically threw Buffy under the bus, saying the murder was all her idea and that she never consulted with him. It was only after she handed him the mortar and pestle and the syringe and told him to dispose of them that he got involved. Personally, I didn't buy it. The timeline was off, but that was for the courts to decide.

Aunt Fern knocked on my apartment door. I could tell it was her because her door had squeaked, and when she stepped on one particular floorboard, it creaked. I leveraged myself off the sofa and opened the door.

She breezed in. "I just found out the sheriff has called a town meeting."

"A town meeting?"

"Yes. We haven't had one of those in years." Aunt Fern almost sounded excited.

I waited for her to tell me more, but clearly she wanted me to ask about it. "You want some tea?"

"No, thank you. I'm too excited."

"Then come sit and tell me all about this meeting."

"I don't know much, but we will be convening in the high school gym since it's the only space large enough for the whole town. I asked Pearl for more details, but even she doesn't know. I don't think the Daniel sisters know either. If Pearl doesn't know, I'm betting Dolly doesn't know either. Though, I wouldn't be surprised if she is withholding information from us. She can be like that sometimes."

I wasn't going to get into that action—ever. "When is this big event?"

"Tomorrow night at nine. Sheriff Duncan wants to make sure everyone can come."

"Which means he's requesting all of the Witch's Cove businesses to close?"

"Yes. They'll have to be if everyone is expected to attend."

"I feel sorry for the tourists."

Aunt Fern nodded. "They'll live. I doubt the meeting will be long."

"I can drive, if you want," I offered.

"That would be great. And let's take Iggy."

What wasn't she telling me? "Why?"

Iggy pranced up to the sofa, crawled up the sofa arm, and settled into Aunt Fern's lap. "Traitor," I said.

"You never invite me anywhere. This could be a huge announcement."

"I refuse to speculate." I couldn't believe that came out of my mouth.

As soon as Aunt Fern returned to her apartment, I called Penny and then Drake. Penny had heard about the meeting, and to my surprise, so had Drake.

"In fact, the sheriff insisted that Jaxson come," Drake said.

That made no sense. "Why? To welcome him to Witch's Cove? That would be a joke."

"I know, right? My brother is staying at my parents' place in Orlando until he figures out his next step. He wasn't happy about being summoned back here."

"Is he going to take the sheriff up on his request?"

"He said he is too curious not to show up."

Now I couldn't wait.

CHAPTER 19

Sheriff Duncan tapped the microphone.

About a thousand of the Witch's Cove residents had shown up, and the bleachers were packed. Penny, her mom, and Tommy were sitting in front of us. I was with Aunt Fern, who had Iggy in her purse, and Drake was on the other side of me, along with Jaxson.

"Thanks for coming on such short notice, but I thought it best to tell you all in person about some events. Sometimes the rumor mill can get a few things wrong," Duncan Donut said.

Aunt Fern leaned toward me. "What rumor mill?"

It took everything I had not to laugh. "Oh, Aunt Fern."

She grinned.

"I have a few things to discuss with you. First is my son's murder." In case there was even one person in the room who didn't know the story, he gave a brief rundown. Somehow the fact that the medical examiner thought Cliff's death was accidental at first never came up. That was okay. I hadn't expected any mention in finding the killer. I suppose it was Penny's clue that led to

Buffy's and Victor's capture, but I liked to think I helped too.

"Secondly," Duncan Donut said. "I need to warn you all about some wolves. As you may recall, Floyd Paxton was killed by a wolf. In all my years in Witch's Cove, I've never seen anything like it. I'm not sure where they came from, but they are here now, so be careful. If your property is fenced in, keep the gate locked."

The crowd murmured their concern. Even I was a little scared, though I'd never heard of wolves walking the beaches at night—full moon or not. On the other hand, our beach was called Moon Bay. Maybe hundreds of years ago, wolves had a home here.

"And for my final announcement: I am retiring." The crowd all talked at once. Duncan Donut was in his sixties, but I thought he'd work forever.

"Did you know about this?" I asked my aunt.

"I had an inkling."

And yet she'd never told me. I eased open the top of her purse. "Did you know, Iggy?"

"My lips are sealed."

I wanted to strangle him.

The sheriff tapped the microphone. "Settle down. We all get old." He smiled and then instantly sobered. "To be honest, eleven years ago I did something I wasn't proud of."

Eleven years ago? All I could think of was the handling of Jaxson's case. Drake grabbed my hand.

The sheriff cleared his throat. "I accused an innocent man of robbing the Liquor Mart. You might remember him. I believe Jaxson Harrison is in the stands. Would you come down here, please?"

I looked over at Drake's brother. His jaw looked like it had turned to steel, and if he'd been a dragon, fire would be shooting out of his nose.

Drake nudged him. "Go on. You've been waiting for this moment forever."

"I'm afraid I might kill him."

"He deserves it, but not when everyone is watching. Go," Drake said.

Thankfully, Jaxson made his way down the aisle to the gym floor. His shoulders were rigid, and his gaze was lasered on Duncan Donut's face. When he approached the sheriff, Duncan Donut faced Jaxson. "I owe this young man an apology. Actually, I owe him more than that. It has eaten away at me all these years, and it's time I come clean." He inhaled. "I've gone to the District Attorney and confessed my part in perpetuating the lie. It is because I didn't tell the truth that I have been stripped of my position as sheriff. I accept that. I deserve it. I'm awaiting the decision as to whether I will have to spend time in jail. In the meantime, the District Attorney is in the process of exonerating Jaxson and expunging his record."

The erupting noise was deafening. I know my heart was beating a rapid tattoo. Drake for sure was thrilled, if the smile on his face was any indication.

When the crowd settled, Jaxson, who looked like he'd been hit by a huge wave, leaned closer to the sheriff. "Why did you lie?"

"I was having an affair with a married woman."

If I thought the crowd was boisterous before, the noise turned into a near roar. The sheriff—or rather the former sheriff—let the crowd get it out of their system before continuing. "I will not name her, but it was wrong of me. When I saw you that night, I panicked."

"Why didn't you just tell me? I wouldn't have said anything."

"I couldn't take the chance."

It was almost as if the two of them were inside a bubble, oblivious to the crowd.

"Do you know who really robbed the liquor store?" Jaxson asked.

Duncan Donut looked down at his shoes for a moment. "Cliff did. I asked him to do it, because I wanted to get rid of you. That will always haunt me. If you wonder why I waited so long to admit my wrong doing, it's because I didn't want to take down my son with me." He held up a hand. "I swear I have towed the line ever since that night, though I know that doesn't make any of it right."

"No, it doesn't."

"I wanted this to be public so that no one in this town will treat you with anything but respect," the sheriff said.

The pressure from Drake's hand intensified to the point of being painful. "Drake?" I whispered.

He looked down and then let go. "Sorry. I can't believe this."

"Me neither."

My fear was that Jaxson might punch out the sheriff in front of the whole town, but thankfully, he didn't.

When the sheriff held out his hand to Jaxson, the whole crowd became deathly silent. Jaxson shook his head, turned around, and rushed out of the gym.

Good for him. I wouldn't have been so easy to forgive either.

I thought Drake would race after him, but he probably understood that his brother needed some time to process this. He'd spent three years in jail for nothing.

Duncan Donut swiped a finger under his eyes and faced the crowd. "I've wanted to say that for so long. I realize that many of you have questions, but I have two other announcements I need to make. As you all know, my son was a father to a three-year old boy named Dusty. Why Cliff withheld this amazing piece of news from me, I don't know nor will I ever know. But I have been in contact with Buffy's parents. They are going to raise their grandson." He held up a hand when the chatter started up again. "The last announcement is that I have asked city council to promote Deputy Steve Rocker to sheriff until an election can be held."

I didn't see that coming, but I was happy for him. Perhaps now if my curiosity got the best of me, I'd have an ally, though fingers crossed, there won't be a next time.

EXCERPT-A PINK POTION GONE WRONG

I hope you enjoyed meeting the townsfolk of Witch's Cove, and Glinda's cute familiar, Iggy, but don't worry, she will be running into trouble soon.

If you want to find out what really happened to Floyd Paxton, check out A Pink Potion Gone Wrong (book 2 of A Witch's Cove Mystery.) Buy on Amazon or read for FREE on Kindle Unlimited

Don't forget to sign up for my Cozy Mystery newsletter *to learn about my discounts and upcoming releases. If you prefer to only receive notices regarding my releases, follow me on BookBub.*

An unlucky witch. A talking pink iguana. A frustrated ghost needing to know who killed him.

Welcome back to Witch's Cove where the people—with the exception of a few random lawbreakers—are friendly and the sun always shines. If you want to talk to a dead relative, learn about your future, or need a spell created just for you, you've come to the right place.

Hi, I'm Glinda Goodall, and after fourteen years of hearing my iguana complain about how my spell turned his green skin pink, I finally have a chance to help him. The problem? I'm either the worst witch in Florida or the unluckiest. At the store where I buy my potions, the owner happened to be out of town. No worries. Why shouldn't I trust the ancient substitute who is hard of hearing and doesn't see well?

Long story short, she mixed in the wrong ingredient, and instead of turning Iggy back to green, I ended up seeing ghosts! Just my luck, the first semi-translucent figure I ran into was recently murdered and wants my help to figure out who did it. Never one to turn down a soul in need, I agree.

If you want to tag along, please do. You'll find me at the Tiki Hut Grill most days serving breakfast and smiles. Oh, yeah. I found a talking cat too!

Enjoy the first chapter of book 2

"I'm on strike," my cute, pink iguana said as he whipped his tail back and forth, digging his claws into the rattan stool he was perched upon. "I'm not helping you with any more cases."

I ignored Iggy, mostly because he was being silly. I'd only been involved in one murder case in my life. But when my familiar was in a bad mood, the best thing to do was give him space to cool down.

To be fair, these last few weeks had been hard on both of us. Me, because I had to help prove that my best male friend's brother didn't kill our not-so-beloved deputy. Iggy had been excited to help solve the crime, but now that the real criminal had been brought to justice, he felt left out. Iggy liked the action.

So why would an adrenaline junkie threaten to boycott

the chance to sleuth in the future? I didn't have a clue, but knowing him, he'd reveal his motives eventually.

Just to be clear, this level of frustration wasn't new to him. Iggy was often in a state of despair, mostly because he was pink (long story how that came about). And by a long story, I mean about fourteen years long.

The short of it was that I had conjured him from the Hendrian National Forest when I was only twelve. Considering my inexperience, it shouldn't come as a surprise that I failed to get the black cat I was trying for. Instead, Iggy showed up—and I turned him pink by mistake. Whoops.

For sure, Iggy got the raw end of the deal. I was a terrible witch back then—still am—because I'm bad at doing spells. It was why I try to limit doing them as much as possible.

"Don't you want to know why I won't help you anymore?" he said, his nose pressed against the picture window that faced the Gulf of Mexico.

I already knew. At least I think I did. He'd complained about being pink almost every day. "No."

"Have you ever asked for help regarding my problem?" he asked.

Nailed it!

Clearly, my familiar wasn't going to let it go. I finished my tea, set it down on the coffee table, and leaned back against the sofa. "If you want to have a discussion, come over here so we can talk face to face."

Claws scraped along the rattan and then along the wood floor. Iggy climbed up on the coffee table and faced me. "I've been begging you to go to the Hex and Bones Apothecary store forever, but you never do. I've heard Mrs. Murdoch is a genius when it comes to finding the right spell. She'll know just what to do to change me back to green."

I had tried to find a solution to his problem, but perhaps I hadn't tried hard enough in Iggy's eyes. "She probably does.

Bertha Murdoch supplies all of the witches with their herbs and stuff." She also had a library of spells, but either I had convinced myself I was too busy to spend hours looking through them all, or else I feared I would mess up again. "What if I change you to some other color, like purple or blue and orange striped? You know my last few spells haven't been raging successes." More like disasters.

"Any color is better than pink. I know your track record isn't the best, but I'm willing to take the chance. I refuse to stay pink any longer." He closed his eyes in rebellion.

Iggy was being particularly anxious, and his bad vibes were beginning to rub off on me. "Why are you bringing this up now?" I held up a hand. "I realize it's on your mind a lot, but many of our town visitors come to the Tiki Hut Grill just to see a pink iguana." I loved him just the way he was.

Iggy opened his eyes and lifted his head. "Tell them to go to the Galapagos."

"You're being childish, though someday I would like to see a real pink iguana."

"A real pink iguana? What, I'm a fake?" Iggy bobbed his head.

"Watch it, buddy. Aggression is not tolerated in this household. Tell me what's really going on."

He stretched out onto his stomach and grunted. "It's bad enough that I feel useless around here, but Aimee made fun of me yesterday for being pink."

"Who the heck is Aimee?" I didn't like anyone bullying my familiar.

He looked away. "My girlfriend."

I had to work hard not to laugh, even though there was nothing funny about romance. "You have a girlfriend?" Iggy had never mentioned he had any interest in the opposite sex.

"Yes." He lifted his head. "Do you have a problem with that?"

"Ah, no, but why haven't I heard about her before now?"

"Do you tell me about your boyfriends?"

I laughed. "What boyfriends?"

Iggy lifted a leg for a moment as if to reach for me. "Okay, your boyfriend. Singular. I know you like Sheriff Rocker."

He was trying to change the subject. "I do not like Sheriff Rocker. Okay, I don't dislike him either, but I don't have any romantic notions about him." Even if I did, I wouldn't tell blabbermouth here.

"I know you think he's hot. I overheard you talking to Penny about him."

Penny was my best girlfriend, who worked with me at the Tiki Hut Grill, and we often chatted about those things. Apparently, I wasn't aware Iggy was close enough to hear us. "I might have mentioned it once or twice. That's all." I needed to get back to Aimee. "Is your girlfriend an iguana?"

"No, she's a cat—the most beautiful black cat I've ever seen."

Ah, so that was the reason for the sudden desire to be green again. "How long have you known her?"

"A week."

A week wasn't a long time, but maybe animals were different when it came to love. "Who is her owner?"

"She doesn't have one."

I crossed my arms over my chest. "You're dating an ordinary cat?"

"No! She's special. Like me. She can talk."

Iggy was losing it. "Tell me this. Can you talk to Toto—an ordinary dog?" That was my mother's dog, who had no magical powers whatsoever. Don't worry, I know that animals communicate in different ways.

Iggy's mouth opened. "You know I can't. Toto is just a dog, but Aimee can really talk."

This was going nowhere. If Aimee could talk, then she

was someone's familiar, which meant she had an owner. "Maybe you can ask her over so I can get to know her."

He shook his head. "When you invite the cute sheriff over here, I'll let you meet Aimee."

I hated when Iggy turned stubborn. "I'll tell you what. I'll go over to Hex and Bones Apothecary right now and see if there is a spell to turn a pink iguana into a green one. How does that sound?"

"Fine." He turned around, his tail swishing at me.

"What? Just fine? I thought you'd be more excited. What else is bugging you?"

He looked over his shoulder. "Like I said, I had so much fun solving Cliff's murder, and now I have nothing to do."

He hadn't actually solved the case. Many people helped bring down the killer, but ever since the case had closed, Iggy had been experiencing this feeling of emptiness. I had to admit, I was too. "You had plenty to do before you helped investigate Cliff's murder."

"Now that I have, I want more."

I sighed. "I get why you feel useless." I snapped my fingers. "Hey, I know. Why don't you apply for a job at the sheriff's department to be a detective?"

I might have been a bit sarcastic there, but it wasn't as if murders happened all that often in Witch's Cove, Florida. We were a small town on the west coast that catered to tourists. Not only did they come for our sandy beaches and endless sunshine, they enjoyed our amazing array of occult services. I have some talents in the witch department, but there weren't any that I might be paid for. For the sake of the town, that was a good thing. I couldn't tell the future or talk to the dead like my mother could.

"If Sheriff Rocker and I could communicate, that would be great, but we can't," Iggy said in his pouty voice. It wasn't attractive.

"There is that." Only witches could talk to other familiars, and Sheriff Rocker didn't qualify. Heck, he barely believed in witches or magic. "Have you ever tried to talk to him? The man could be a closet warlock." I almost laughed out loud at that thought.

"Funny, funny. We both know he's not."

"I just thought maybe I'd misjudged him." Sometimes Iggy figured things out before I did.

My familiar faced me once more and lifted the upper half of his body, looking like a sentry. "I thought you said you were going."

It was important that I show him that he was really important to me, and that I cared for his mental well-being. "I am."

I stood, shoved my credit card in my pocket and headed downstairs. Instead of leaving by the side entrance that ran through the Tiki Hut gift store, I passed through the main restaurant.

Was I being crazy for attempting this spell? Some spells I'd tried had been fairly innocuous, so if I messed up, it was no big deal. Others, however, would have had dire consequences if I'd failed—like the spell I did to find Iggy.

It was my day off from waitressing, so I had the time to ask Bertha about the ins and outs of this spell.

"Glinda, is everything okay?" Aunt Fern asked as I rushed by the checkout counter she was manning. "You look worried."

I never could fool my aunt. I stopped and backed up. After glancing around and then waving to Penny, I returned my focus to her. "Not really. Iggy is in a funk."

She set down her wand—or rather her pencil that looked like a wand. "Because he feels useless?"

"He told you?"

She tapped the side of her fairy godmother crown. "I

know how hard it is when people need you, and then they don't."

Was she talking about Iggy or herself? I didn't need to get into that discussion at the moment.

"Yes, he's upset that he can no longer play detective, but he's also upset because his new girlfriend prefers him to be green instead of pink."

"Aimee?"

Really? "Is there anything you don't know?" While there was no such thing as mental telepathy—or so I believed—I wouldn't be surprised if she and Iggy communicated that way.

My aunt smiled. "I'm sure there is. Where are you headed in such a hurry?"

"I'm going to Hex and Bones Apothecary."

Aunt Fern grinned. "How exciting. Are you going to return to your witchy ways?" She wiggled her eyebrows.

I huffed out a laugh. "I have no witchy ways. Any magical abilities I possess have gone haywire too often to even call me a real witch."

"Nonsense. Bertha will not steer you wrong. Just follow her directions, and I'm sure Iggy will be green in no time."

My shoulders slumped. "For his sake, I want him to be green, but to be honest, I like him pink. It's what makes him unique."

My aunt shook her head. "You have to think what's best for him."

"I know. It's why I finally agreed to find a solution after all this time."

My aunt patted my hand. "You're doing the right thing."

"I hope so. How's Uncle Harold today, by the way?" I didn't ask often enough, but truth be told, he'd died over two years ago.

Aunt Fern claimed his ghostly body appeared most days

to talk to her. I personally didn't believe in ghosts, mainly because I'd never seen one, but if she said he could communicate with her, then maybe ghosts did exist.

"He's weak. It takes energy to materialize enough for me to see him. He said he needed to rest for a few days."

My stomach cramped. "Oh, no." I couldn't ask if his condition was terminal, because he was already dead. "I probably should have asked before, but does this happen often?"

Aunt Fern tilted her head once more and smiled. When her fairy godmother hat slipped, she righted it. "Oh, yes, but don't worry. He'll be right as rain soon."

I never did understand how rain could be right or wrong, but I let it drop. "I'll let you know how the spell for Iggy goes."

"You do that."

Contrary to popular opinion, just because she wore a fairy godmother outfit most days to work, she was not crazy. The ghost part? Maybe, but all employees—and owner as was the case with my aunt—at the Tiki Hut Grill wore a costume. The tourists loved it. I always dressed up as Glinda the Good Witch of the South, because I am a witch (albeit a fairly unsuccessful one), and I live in the south.

Aunt Fern occasionally alternated her costume, depending on her mood, but the godmother one was her favorite. I swear she chose this one because so many people spilled their deepest, darkest secrets to her just because of how she looked—sweet and trusting.

I stepped outside and immediately wilted. It was a hot June day. The silver lining was that there were enough clouds to keep me from sweating too much on the short walk to the Hex and Bones store down the road. I crossed the street and walked past the sheriff's department, working hard not to look inside. Once Steve Rocker had become the new sheriff, after Sheriff Duncan had retired—or rather had been forced to step down—I hadn't seen much of him. According to some of our second shift servers, the new sheriff usually came into the Tiki Hut for dinner, but since I had the breakfast and lunch shift, I rarely saw him.

I suppose I could have gone over to see how he was settling into the town, but I felt it would look a little suspicious. When Cliff Duncan had been murdered, Steve Rocker and I crossed paths many times—sometimes on friendly terms and at other times, not so much. While he was skeptical that I could detect how a person died, he had started to come around to my way of thinking just when he—or rather we—solved Cliff's murder.

Refocusing on the task at hand, I hurried to the apothecary shop. Once inside, I was immediately assaulted with what smelled like a combination of dust, coriander, and some other strong odor. Because the tourists expected it, there was a table with jars of bones and skulls of all shapes and sizes just inside the main entrance—all plastic knock offs, of course. Besides the usual witchy trinkets, the shop had a wall of herbs and spices, all in different sized colored containers. Each one was numbered and labeled.

Stars, moons, and ancient symbols that meant nothing to me hung by colored threads from the ceiling. Most were swaying since the air conditioner was at full blast. While some things in the store were a bit too touristy for me, the ambience of the place oozed the occult.

The catchy store's name made it ripe to sell clothing apparel with the Hex and Bones logo. Even though it was months before Halloween, the store always kept a section dedicated to dressing as a witch—or what the world thought a witch should look like. They had black hats, striped stockings, wands, and even a few black gowns. And yes, an assortment of brooms. I always got a kick out of that.

Next to that section was the candle display. I loved candles, but Bertha's were rather expensive since they were handmade. Along one side wall sat tables with ancient looking, leather bound books on them. These books contained spells and folklore. According to the owner, everything in them was authentic. It was where I might be able to find the spell to help Iggy.

"May I help you?" said a wobbly voice behind me.

I spun around, expecting to see Bertha. Instead, Hazel Silas, an ancient witch, was standing there, her shoulders hunched. I waited for her to recognize me, but when she didn't, I introduced myself. "I'm Glinda Goodall, Fern's niece." I didn't ask if she remembered me since I didn't want to embarrass her in case she didn't. We had met a few times.

"Oh, yes. You work at the Tiki Hut."

Good. She did remember. "I do." I scanned the store once more. "I'm looking for Bertha."

"I'm sorry, dear, Bertha is visiting her ill sister in Atlanta."

"That's terrible—about her sister being sick, that is. When will she be back?" I wasn't sure how long Iggy would be willing to wait.

"She doesn't know. It could be days. It could be weeks."

Decisions, decisions. If I had the ingredients in hand, it might put off Iggy for a while. "Maybe you can help me then. I need to do a spell."

Hazel's smile faltered. "Oh? What kind of spell?"

"I need to turn my pink iguana back to green."

Buy on Amazon or read for FREE on Kindle Unlimited
 THE END

OTHER BOOKS BY THE AUTHOR

THE TIME TRAVEL TALISMAN COZY MYSTERY (Cozy Mystery)
The Knitting Conundrum (book 1)
The Knitting Dilemma (book 2)
The Knitting Enigma (book 3)
The Knitting Quandary (book 4)

A WITCH'S COVE MYSTERY (Paranormal Cozy Mystery)
PINK Is The New Black (book 1)
A PINK Potion Gone Wrong (book 2)
The Mystery of the PINK Aura (book 3)
Box Set (books 1-3)
Sleuthing In The PINK (book 4)
Not in The PINK (book 5)
Gone in the PINK of an Eye (book 6)
Box Set (books 4-6)
The PINK Pumpkin Party (book 7)
Mistletoe with a PINK Bow (book 8)
The Magical PINK Pendant (book 9)

Box Set (books 7-9)
The Poisoned PINK Punch (book 10)
PINK Smoke and Mirrors (book 11)
Broomsticks and PINK Gumdrops (book 12)
Box Set (books 10-12)
Knotted Up In PINK Yarn (book 13)
Ghosts and PINK Candles (book 14)
Pilfered PINK Pearls (book 15)
Box Set (books 13-15)
The Case of the Stolen PINK Tombstone (book 16)
The PINK Christmas Cookie Caper (book 17)
PINK Moon Rising (book 18)
Box set(books 16-18)
The PINK Wedding Dress Whodunit (book 19)

SILVER LAKE SERIES (3 OF THEM)
<u>A TASTE OF SILVER LAKE</u>
Weres and Witches Box Set (books 1-2)
Hidden Realms Box Set (books 1-2)
Goddesses of Destiny Box Set (books 1-2)
(1). **<u>HIDDEN REALMS OF SILVER LAKE</u>** (Paranormal Romance)
Awakened By Flames (book 1)
Seduced By Flames (book 2)
Box Set (books 1-2)
Kissed By Flames (book 3)
Destiny In Flames (book 4)
Box Set (books 3-4)
Passionate Flames (book 5)
Ignited By Flames (book 6)
Box Set (books 5-6)
Touched By Flames (book 7)
Bound By Flames (book 8)
Box set (books 7-8)

Fueled By Flames (book 9)
Scorched By Flames (book 10)
Box Set (books 9-10)

(2). **GODDESSES OF DESTINY** Paranormal Romance)
Slade (book 1)
Rafe (book 2)
Will (book 3)
Josh (book 4)
Jace (book 5)
Tanner (book 6)

(3). **WERES AND WITCHES OF SILVER LAKE** (Paranormal Romance)
A Magical Shift (book 1)
Catching Her Bear (book 2)
Surge of Magic (book 3)
The Bear's Forbidden Wolf (book 4)
Box Set (books 1-4)

Her Reluctant Bear (book 5)
Freeing His Tiger (book 6)
Protecting His Wolf (book 7)
Waking His Bear (book 8)
Box Set (books 5-8)
Melting Her Wolf's Heart (book 9)
Her Wolf's Guarded Heart (book 10)
His Rogue Bear (book 11)
Reawakening Their Bears (book 12)
Box Set (books 9-12)

OTHER PARANORMAL SERIES

PACK WARS (Paranormal Romance)

Training Their Mate (book 1)
Claiming Their Mate (book 2)
Rescuing Their Virgin Mate (book 3)
Box Set (books 1-3)
Loving Their Vixen Mate (book 4)
Fighting For Their Mate (book 5)
Enticing Their Mate (book 6)
Box Set (books 4-6)
Their Huntress Mate (book 7)
Craving Their Mate (book 8)

PACK WARS-THE GRANGERS
Meant for them (book 1)
Meant for wolves (book 2)
Meant for forever (book 3)
Meant for her (book 4)

HIDDEN HILLS SHIFTERS (Paranormal Romance)
An Unexpected Diversion (book 1)
Bare Instincts (book 2)
Shifting Destinies (book 3)
Embracing Fate (book 4)
Promises Unbroken (book 5)
Bare 'N Dirty (book 6)
Hidden Hills Shifters Complete Box Set (books 1-6)

CONTEMPORARY SERIES
MONTANA PROMISES (Full length contemporary Romance)
Promises of Mercy (book 1)
Foundations For Three (book 2)
Montana Fire (book 3)
Montana Promises Box Set (books 1-3)
Hart To Hart (Book 4)

Burning Seduction (Book 5)
Montana Promises Complete Box Set (books 1-5)
Novellas:
Montana Desire (book 1)
Awakening Passions (book 2)

PLEDGED TO PROTECT (contemporary romantic suspense)
From Panic To Passion (book 1)
From Danger To Desire (book 2)
From Terror To Temptation (book 3)

BURIED SERIES (contemporary romantic suspense)
Buried Alive (book 1)
Buried Secrets (book 2)
Buried Deep (book 3)
The Buried Series Complete Box Set (books 1-3)

A NASH MYSTERY (Contemporary Romance)
Sidearms and Silk (book 1)
Black Ops and Lingerie (book 2)
A Nash Mystery Box Set (books 1-2)

STARTER SETS (Romance)
Contemporary
Paranormal

ABOUT THE AUTHOR

Author Bio

Love it HOT and STEAMY? Sign up for my newsletter and receive MONTANA DESIRE for FREE. Click here

OR Are you a fan of quirky PARANORMAL COZY MYSTERIES? Sign up for this newsletter. Click Here

Not only do I love to read, write, and dream, I'm an extrovert. I enjoy being around people and am always trying to understand what makes them tick. Not only must my romance books have a happily ever after, I need characters I can relate to. My men are wonderful, dynamic, smart, strong, and the best lovers in the world (of course).

. . .

My Paranormal Cozy Mysteries are where I let my imagination run wild with witches and a talking pink iguana who believes he's a real sleuth.

I believe I am the luckiest woman. I do what I love and I have a wonderful, supportive husband, who happens to be hot!

Fun facts about me

(1) I'm a math nerd who loves spreadsheets. Give me numbers and I'll find a pattern.
   (2) I live on a Costa Rica beach!
   (3) I also like to exercise. Yes, I know I'm odd.

I love hearing from readers either on FB or via email (hint, hint).

Social Media Sites

Website: www.velladay.com
   FB: www.facebook.com/vella.day.90
   Twitter: velladay4

Printed in Great Britain
by Amazon